Beware of the D

Beware of the D

Mr Oh

Mr Oh

2018

First Printing: 2018

ISBN 978-0-244-06150-0

www.MrOh.co.uk

Ordering Information:
Special discounts are available on quantity purchases by corporations, associations, educators, and others. For details, contact the publisher at the above listed address.

U.S. trade bookstores and wholesalers: Please contact Mr Oh via email:
misterohyes@gmail.com

Acknowledgements

To anyone who has read any of my books, supported or even represented for my work, I appreciate you from my heart bottom.

I've been doing this writing thing for 17 years and this is the first book I've written and released in the space of two months. I had the idea for this story in November 2017 as a short story that people were gonna be able to read on my website. But the more I wrote, the more I liked it. SO I kept writing and by New Year's Day, I finished it. And I wanted it out.

So here we are.

I hope you like it. It's just a story and I hope, whether you like it or not, you are able to get into it. If something makes you laugh, sigh, moan, giggle, groan like 'ohhhh a woman would never do that', anything you do as a result of reading this book then I've done my job as a writer.

To the ACTUAL thank yous: Thank you Lee for snapping an amazing front and back cover (lacenquiries@gmail.com), Daniel Edwards the model (Insta - @Senpai_d247), thanks to Simone inspiring me with her name, Miss D for letting me hide in her room to write, Marcia for letting me use the peace and quiet of her yard to write and my new favourite place All You Read Is Love where most of this story was written (if you ever go there, get the banana and pecan cake). Thank you to the queen of everything for her constant support and encouraging words (You know who you are) and to anyone who has read the snippets I put out.

Most of all, thanks to you the reader. If you've got this far, you've invested in this story and I just hope you like it.

For more information, check out www.mroh.co.uk

Instagram: misterohhhhh

Twitter: MrOhYes

Facebook: Mista Oh

Foreword

My name is Simone Denise McKenzie…

Thursday 1st February 2018

$imone: The heating is on, I'm in a onesie with a dressing gown on, sliders on and I'm STILL cold. Fuck February.

Katt: Are you sure that's the only reason you hate February?

$imone: YES IT IS!

Katt: The caps say otherwise.

B: Leave my sister alone!

Katt: You're sister is hungry!

Russia: Especially in February!

And here we go again!

I'm sitting on my extra large comfy sofa, dressed like I wanted to move to the Arctic Circle and my girls are making me want to come off my phone and bury my head in the sand. One, because they were right - I hate February - and two, I could feel them getting shady over my dick-less existence.

And dick-less in February!?

Thus the shade.

Quiet What's App, no-one hunting around my DMs and the only fun messages I get are internet-only deals from lastminute and boohoo.com.

Don't get it twisted, I'm not like some lonely leper, I work. And I work HARD!

I've got a life, you know? I've got a social life, I'm all up in the gym and I've got my girls so I'm not like a sad case or nothing like that.

My phone vibrated in my lap as the Nollywood film I was watching ended with an absolutely awful cover of Whitney

Houston's *I Will Always Love You.*

As always, the shade hit deep but I never let them know. They did it all the time and thought it was funny. I took it but I always gave it back.

In fact, hold on...

I picked up my phone, which had slipped under my M&Ms cover I had draped on my legs on the sofa.

Opening my What's App group chat, I started to think of possible retorts.

The girls had graduated to full shade while my sister, Brina, stayed busy trying to defend me. Not that she had much to defend.

I mean, the shade WAS warranted but that's neither here nor there.

$imone: Leave me and my cobweb thighs alone!

Russia: You said it not me.

Katt: Looooooooool!

$imone: It's okay, I use my money to fan the webs away!

B: CHA CHING!

Russia: Yeah but money isn't that dick that you can feel in your stomach.

Katt: This one dick I had the other day, I swear I couldn't walk.

Resting my head on my hand with a heavy sigh, I couldn't help remembering the last time I had that feeling in my stomach. A dick reaching and pounding inside me so much that I feel like he's reaching my pasta lunch from the afternoon.

I can be honest with you, right? Yes YOU the reader and I'd never tell my girls this, but I got so frustrated at that moment I actually kicked my cover off my feet. My one bedroom flat in Greenwich was covered in low light from a tall lamp in the corner and my glass of wine was annoyingly out of reach on a table in the middle of my living room.

Russia: How long HAS it been Mone?
$imone is typing…
B: Tell em sis. Tell em you got some dick last week.
Katt: Nah, it's been at LEAST three months.

I wasn't typing anything, I was just looking for the middle finger emoji which I added 17 times before deleting.

And for the record, I got dick last night. And it was good! Rocked my world, knocked my socks off and I swear, there is no-one better! Granted he's not attached to anyone, his name is Bob and I keep him in my bedside drawer but I gets mines. I'm not even gonna type that… they know I've got a special attachment to my friend.

A real dick though? A real, thick, lengthy, veiny, slides in with a little bit of pain dick? That answer is seven months, three weeks and 13 days and counting.

B: Don't worry sis, I got you covered. Prick face says he's knows this guy at work who's looking for someone to do.

Katt: That's what you need, a friend with benefits.

Russia: I've got a few. I can lend you a dick or two.

$imone: Erm, I don't want none of your hoodrat dick thanks.

Russia: Don't discount the hood dick. Some of the best

dick comes out the ends.

Katt: Yeah STDs too!

B: Loool... remember that time?

Katt: We don't need to bring that back up.

$imone: LMAOOOOOOOO

Russia: I remember, she text me like 'MY PUSSY IS ON FIRE!'

B: Looooooooooooooooool

Katt: The joke was, it felt good before the burning sensation.

$imone: Yeah, I'm good thanks... sis talk to me.

B: Don't worry, I've already given him your number.

$imone: WTF?!

My eyes opened wide and I sat up in the corner of the sofa and grabbed my phone with both hands. I was going to need both thumbs for this cussing.

$imone: Fuck off! You best be joking sis

B: Nah for real, he's a nice guy, I met him once

Russia: Show me a pic so I know it's real

Katt: OoOoOoOo, don't be mad Mone, get you some.

Russia: You notice she didn't tell us how long it's been?

$imone: Nah, you know I don't like giving my number out to people especially some random guy your whore of a husband works with.

Katt: Whore of a husband ya kna!

B: Yeah but he is! We all know it!

Russia: So why do you stay with him?

$imone: Watch she's gonna say 'because I love him'?

Katt: I'm still laughing at 'whore of a husband'.

I suddenly felt watched, like someone was watching me. Such was the feeling knowing that someone had my number and I didn't give it to them.

I work very hard so I don't get a lot of play a lot. After every break up, I'd change my number just to avoid that returning 'hey big head' text. If you had my phone number, I wanted you to have it so my sister's apparent decision to give my number out wasn't sitting well with me. All I kept thinking was: 'so this random dude is gonna call me out of the blue? For fuck sake!'

B: Look you need some dick, he needs some pussy. Just be grown and get yours.

Russia: Yeah Sim, it's been long enough.

Katt: Is he blessed?

B: How do I know? Prick face didn't touch his dick to find out.

$imone: When are you gonna leave him?

B: This ain't about me, it's about you getting an orgasm before Valentines Day.

$imone: But I don't care about Valentines Day and all those pagan holidays. I never have you know that.

Katt: Then care about getting some dick in ya belly.

B: Yeah sis, he's a nice guy. Just be real and try not to freeze him out.

$imone: I'm not cold, I just can't be bothered to find a man who will eventually flop and fuck up my life.

Russia: You need to stop thinking that's all they do.

$imone: Yeah but you lot are always complaining about men and how they fuck up.

Katt: Yeah but pussy isn't an alternative so how can we replace them?

I thought about my bedside drawer and smiled.

B: He says he's gonna message you in a minute, Prick Face said.

$imone: I'm not taking any notice. I don't know him and I didn't give him my number so I'm not even entertaining this STRANGER. Trust me. I am not renting out my tuntun just to get an orgasm from someone I don't even know.

Russia: Erm, okaay Iyala. It doesn't have to be that deep. It's just sex.

It's not just sex though. It's the meeting of physical vessels, the merging of souls and energies.

That shit IS deep!

Not any and everyone gets to ride this train I'm afraid.

Russia: What's his name?

Katt: Yeah, what's the dick's name?

B: Andre.

I froze reading the name. So the mystery dick that was about to call was the namesake of one of my favourite artists in the world?

Didn't mean anything but I caught the link.

I said my goodbyes to the girls and came out of our group, tossing my phone onto the closest cushion.

Reaching for it again, I checked that it wasn't set on silent just in case I missed his message. Then I stopped and reminded myself.

'Like I care anyway,' I mumbled and threw my phone back on the sofa.

Just then my phone vibrated with a microwave sound effect and my neck snapped in its direction.

As much as I am trying to act cool, there is a strange excitement running through me. My sister knows full well how private and slightly introverted I am so it's a nervous excitement. I don't like strangers. Well, people. That's another story.

Katt: Have a nice one bitches!

$imone: A bitch ain't a hole for a man to feel...

B: A bitch is a beauty in tremendously cute heels.

Katt: Eyyy eyyyyyyy eyyyyyyyyy!

Russia: Can't believe you lot still say that. My girl died time ago.

$imone: But Blue lives forever.

Katt: Let us know how it goes.

I locked my phone, turned off the TV, shuffled to my bedroom and got into bed as per my regular, set bedtime.

Slipping out of my onesie, draping my duvet over me, I kicked my feet as my sheets attempted to chill my toes. Checking my alarms were set for the next morning, I checked my notifications, telling myself I wasn't waiting for a stranger.

And that's when I got the first What's App message.

Friday 2nd February 2018

Let me tell you about how cold and tired I am right now. Because the combination of the two is pissing me off!

February isn't the month for skirts and bare legs, that's for sure!

The cold is because February can suck it's mudda from a distance. The tiredness is because a few minutes after you left me last night, my phone beeped and my sister's husband's friend messaged me.

Andre his name is! And, well, I didn't go to bed until 6am.

My usual bedtime is 10.30pm but that all went out the window when he sent the first message which said: 'Are you the woman who's looking for some fair, honest penis?'

The introduction message had me laughing my ass off in my bed. I was laying there hoping I'd fall asleep before the message arrived but the honesty in his intro intrigued me.

Dubious and unsure on whether or not to answer, I responded with a smiling emoji and it all started from there.

So, my sister really DID tell this man I needed some dick! He told me the same thing word for word. I was shocked and found it funny at the same time. While messaging her to call her "an adopted mistake that should've been swallowed", I was swapping back to messages from Andre which, thank God, weren't the usual crap messages like 'wha'gwan, what you saying, what's the motive?'

God I hate men that talk like that! Grown ass men who feel like their bodies have grown but their levels of speech have not gone through puberty yet. Those guys who say four words before switching to sex talk in the hope of getting sent a picture or two.

FUCK OFF MATE!

Now this Andre... this guy had me up WAYYY past my bedtime and we didn't talk about sex once. Okay, that's a lie we did mention it but after that we talked about everything else but. We talked about music, food, TV, Brexit, the apocalypse that is Theresa May... okay not everything, felt like it though.

And he knew his shit too. He didn't SOUND like someone who was trying to talk his way into my panties or keep up by sounding intelligent. By the end of the conversation I was really interested in his opinion.

Then the awkward part of the convo kicked in. Awkward because I'd warmed to him.

Andr3: So, sex huh?
$imone: Yeah.
Andr3: Want some?
$imone: Sure
Andr3: Okay, we should set that up.
$imone: Whenever you're ready

Even as I said the words, I tried to suck them back into my mouth but I'd already sent them. Honestly, they felt quite comfy dropping into the conversation and I waited for his response, which was a brief itinerary of his movements for the following week. That sparked a conversation about Christmas which opened a can of worms about religion and that kept us on the phone for another three hours.

As I said I'm tired!

The boy sure can talk but he listened too, a rarity in men I find but hey. It was nice.

The bin liner bags under my eyes are not sexy at all though.

Lemme tell you just how late I went to bed. I hung up, set my alarm and 20 minutes later, the alarm went off.

Yeah I look and feel like shit! And today's such an important day as well.

The production company I work for are having a table read of their, well my next project, which is a documentary about legendary criminal Tatiana Blue. I was still pushing for a positive spin on her presence and what she did for the normal everyday woman but they thought such a tone was a reach. The doc had been given the green light by Channel 4 and had been cast for extras but today was the reading of the character part of the documentary. And I had to be there early to set up the conference room for the Channel 4 execs who were coming down.

And as you are reading this, I'm still 10 minutes away from work. My phone had been blowing up from my boss asking where I am and Andre is up and has been making me laugh as I take pigeon steps on snow-covered pavements.

I stopped off at Tesco Express, picking up some juices and snacks so my boss would think I was late picking up snacks and drinks for the table read.

It worked as he apologised to me as soon as I walked in and he saw the bags in my hands.

My curved cluttered desk greeted me with a confused smile and I sat down with a heavy sigh. I unwrapped my scarf from my neck, took over my gloves and didn't know where to start first. My desk was full of storyboards, rewrites from the day before, song ideas I had for the documentary and random other shit.

Placing my handbag on my desk, I felt my phone vibrate and searched through my bag for it.

It was a message from Andre. Immediately I smiled.

Hearing his voice in my ears for well over six hours gave a certain weight to whatever he sent me. Geez, we talked for the equivalent of a work shift.

I opened the message and was instantly intrigued, shocked, disgusting and thirsty at the same time.

Andr3: Good morning Simone. Talking to you last night was definitely an interesting moment in time. To say that I'm not interested in meeting you would be the biggest lie. I'm glad we've been able to be honest with each other so it won't make my next comment so crazy.

I reclined my chair, ignoring everyone in the office and slouching low so no-one would pay me any attention. I read on with interest.

Andr3: I've booked a hotel. I'm actually staying at a hotel for work purposes but I'm done for the day and, well, it's my last night here so I thought I'd shoot my shot. I'm staying at the Novotel Hotel in Canary Wharf.

My first instinctive emotion was disgust like, 'am I just some any random tramp he could take to a hotel and fuck?'

That was my initial feeling. A warm tingling sensation that started in my tummy and trailed down between my thighs followed and I read on.

Andr3: I'm not trying to treat you like some any woman. I

just had an idea and thought fuck it shoot your shot. If you're interested, I'll leave a key at reception for you. It's room 2290 on the 22nd floor.

I locked my phone and hugged it to my chest with a smile. I was judging myself for the fact that this guy had me even thinking about spending a night with him after one night of conversation, some of which was spent talking about what we liked and disliked sexually. That section of the conversation was a lot for me as his voice took a deeper tone and he explained in detail how he hadn't been with anyone in over a year and missed the intimacy. I personally didn't believe him. He probably just missed pussy and wanted to get his dick wet. That's not to say I wasn't hungry too because... bwoooooiiiii, it's been a minute.

Let's just say... I've worn out three toys in six weeks and have a month's supply of double A batteries on hand at all times.

'So... he wants to do a hotel, motel, holiday inn?' I asked myself with my phone clutched to my chest.

My thoughts were full of skin-to-skin, hands running through my hair, palm on my ass moments with the lights of Canary Wharf lighting the night sky.

Suddenly my desk phone rang, jumping me out of my singy-songy groove I was starting to whine my waist to.

'Sim's gonna get some diiiiiiii... hello?' I said answering the phone. 'Yeah I'll be right there!'

Hanging up the phone with a massive sigh, I gathered a few files and folders from my bag, combined them with some folders from my desk and made my way to the conference meeting room where an announcement was due.

I'll catch up with you afterwards because this is an important meeting but it's gonna be really fucking boring though.

It's now 9pm and I'm walking across South Quay footbridge in Zara heels and a faux fur jacket draped across my body. Of COURSE I decided to go. After the meeting, Andre sent me pictures of the hotel and I was sold. From the moment I knew I was going to go, I got my sister on the phone and did as many checks on him as I could. Brina told me she'd only met him once and he seemed like a nice guy. It wasn't enough but she said her husband vouched for him. Brina's husband was definitely not trustworthy but he's another story.

I got home from work, put my bags down and read over every message he sent me, still undecided at that point. The honesty we shared about our non-existent sex lives made me feel like we'd cut out the bullshit and gone straight to a strange comfort and understanding.

The picture he sent last night scrolled onto my screen and I hummed and bit my lip.

'Chaaaaa, who knows, get an orgasm… hopefully!'

And here I am, following the GPS on my phone to a hotel I could see from the train station. I'd gone for a simple knee-length dress I ordered from ASOS and heels and my black fur running down to my ankles. Big hand bag hiding my change of clothes and toiletries. February was sending drastically cold whistles at my ankles which made me hold one arm across my chest and my phone hand close to my face. According to the map, I was three minutes away and nerves suddenly flushed over me as I took a misstep.

I was going to meet a man I didn't know nor had I ever met before for unknown sex. It could be good, bad, weird, he could be a…

At that moment I stopped walking, came out of my maps app and sent a message to my girl's group.

$imone: If anyone needs me, I'm at the Novotel Hotel in Canary Wharf. Don't ask me no questions about what I'm doing. Tea in the morning.

I sent the message, put my phone on silent and went back to my maps app to make sure I wasn't tempted to read and reply to their obvious messages wondering what I was going to be doing at the hotel and with who. I knew my girls would put two and two together and make four (minus one that's three quick maths) and I'm sure Brina would fill in any blanks.

That big mouth sister of mine.

On a long stretch of road, shaded by an overhead DLR track, I could see the hotel and the cold, coupled with my nerves, had me physically shaking.

Of course I was nervous! What if he was a serial killer or a member of an elite human trafficking group and he needed someone on the thicker side for their books. I pressed my wrist against my jacket pocket to feel for a small pen knife attached to my house keys just in case.

The hotel was a massive, beautiful structure in the middle of a built-up, highly populated area of tall buildings and skyscrapers. Construction sites were sprinkled along the way, promising the best in two and three bedroom living for true London bollocks prices.

'Shit!' I mumbled to my phone as Andre called and interrupted the maps app.

I took a deep breath and answered, channelling my inner Jill Scott.

'Hello,' I tried to be as seductive as I could.

'Good evening to you. How are you?'

'Cold,' I said with a shiver, though his voice instantly warmed me.

'Excellent. Well if you're cold, that means you're outside. Does that mean that you are on your way here?'

I couldn't help the smile on my face. 'I'm literally outside.'

'Really? Oh, okay, well let me fix myself up and put some clothes on.'

My eyebrows raised high and I was instantly drawn into a daydream of what his body could look like. With only facial pictures shared, I hadn't seen his body but having carried my ass all this way, I was more than intrigued to see it for real.

I wanted to speak but my daydream had gone beneath his belly button.

'Hello? HELLO? I said do you want me to come down and meet you.'

'Oh shit, erm, yeah okay.'

'Alright, see you in a minute.'

'Okay, see you soon. Bye.'

His voice was gone but there was an obvious effect leftover as I felt my nipples tighten against my H&M bra, which I needed to throw away because fuck H&M!

Nerves were fighting horny in a back and forth civil war

and I was walking jelly. My legs didn't feel like my own, I was suddenly getting really hot and I couldn't stop smiling.

Rounding the hotel, through cross archways and spot lights on the ground, I took in the decor with a wow. Really nice place if you ever have enough money to go. I had a look on booking.com and found out that a room for two nights started at £165 per night. Much more than my bank account was set up for at the moment.

'I wonder what he looks like in person,' I said to myself as I pushed through a revolving door.

Dance music and elderflower. Those were the two things my senses took in.

White people were everywhere which instantly told me there was money in this hotel. Swirling stairs, wood panel walls, seats swinging from the ceiling... this shit is fancy for real. And this was just the reception.

Trying not to look like a tourist, I parked my rear in a comfy chair that looked like a throne and turned to face the lifts. I crossed my legs, letting my jacket fall open but making sure not to give away the farm.

Sitting for two minutes, I checked my phone and could see I had plenty notifications from my girls but didn't read what they were saying.

Something changed suddenly and I looked up as Andre turned out of a lift and walked towards me.

FUCKING CHOCOLATE! (I swear a lot by the way.)

My hand covered my mouth as if I said it out loud.

I giggled straight after and stood up as he smiled at me.

'Well HELLO Miss Simone!' were his first words but I didn't hear anything. I was too busy watching his lips move.

Low fade, pure shiny chocolate skin, bloody beautiful smile, juicy beard, white teeth… FUCK ME!

The kid is handsome!

'Hi Andre, nice to meet you.'

I went with formal to hide how excited my body had become all of a sudden but he curved my handshake and hugged me. His hands slid into my jacket and round my waist and my spine straightened up. He dipped under my arms and squeezed me in a way that made me inhale deeply.

I had to let him go! Listen, in that hug, I HAD to let him go.

Because BWOOOOOIIIIIII… I tingled.

'You hungry? You want something to eat or drink?'

He needed to stop talking to me! I just got lost in the way his lips moved. And his soft, neat beard smelled like coconut oil.

'No, I'm okay thanks.'

Internally, the civil war of nerves and horny had become an all-out massacre.

'Okay that's fine. We can get room service if you want something later.'

LATER!

Hearing that word made my nerves jump to the forefront and the whole situation made me scared. What if I didn't know what to do with a dick? What if I'd lost the arch in my back? Did I even know how to enjoy sucking a dick any more?

'Well I'm ready when you are,' Andre said with his arm

leading towards the lifts.

'Oh okay,' I stumbled over myself, closed my jacket and walked towards the lift, feeling him watching me as my heels clopped on the floor. I gave my hips a nervous swish and I heard him hum.

And that's when my nerves shut everything down.

Saturday 3rd February 2018

Shhhhhhhh!!!

Okay, I have to be quiet because a certain someone is sleeping. Trust me he deserves the sleep.

I'm sitting on the toilet in a very sexy hotel room. Don't worry, I'm not peeing... I just needed to come in here and let you know what the hell happened.

\`

First of all, Andre is an absolute DEMON!

When my nerves shut me down and I stopped walking to the lifts, he put a hand on the small of my back and held me.

'Are you okay?' he said on some smooth Boyz II Men deep voice shit. I sure did hear him that time.

'Yeah, I just got a bit light headed.'

'D'you wanna sit down for a second?'

'No, I want to go upstairs.'

OoOooo I swear I sounded as smooth as Beyonce as I said that while fighting off an almost debilitating bout of nerves. The look on his face said everything I wanted it to and he led the way. We didn't share any words on the way up, just stood next to each other with our arms rubbing against each other.

Reaching the 22nd floor, he set off first and I followed, watching him walk. Broad shoulders, bit of definition in the back of his arms and a lot of chocolate. His t-shirt stretched nicely across his back and I was happy to take in the air of whatever he aftershave he had on.

We got in the room, he closed the door and that was the moment it became real for me.

I sat on the bed then imagined the things we could do on it and I got up instantly and took a swirling chair instead.

Nothing was calming my nerves as I watched him move around the room in tracksuit bottoms and t-shirt looking like a snack. I wanted to move back to the bed but I didn't want my moving around to appear as uncomfortable as I felt.

And that was it! We didn't do anything!

I couldn't get off the chair. We talked and continued the same vibe we had on the phone but I couldn't take myself to the bed. I was just too nervous. He'd made himself comfortable as we watched film after random TV show but not getting any closer to the fucking that I really wanted.

So, we went to bed. After the fourth or fourteenth episode of *The Big Bang Theory*, he requested I get changed into my bed clothes. He did it so politely, I went into the bathroom and got changed.

I'd only packed my sexy nightie I ordered from Ann Summers and it felt out of place. I imagined we'd be fucking up and down the room by now and the black silky number would be crumpled on the floor somewhere. But I put it on same way. My body was gym fit with healthy curves in the right places so I worked it.

And then... we went to bed.

We left the TV on and he spooned behind me and that

was it.

Until about 1am in the morning.

I instantly woke out of my sleep. Can't remember if I was dreaming or what but I just jumped out of my sleep and his arm was wrapped around my waist. And his dick was nestled nicely between my cheeks.

It'd been a LONG time since I'd woke up to that feeling and let me tell you, I wasn't nervous any more.

I WAS wet though.

If I was having a dream, it must've been a good one because with the smallest of movements, his dick separated my lips just a little bit.

A movement I liked. But Andre was still asleep.

Annoying as I was ready to throw all caution out of the window and grasp the dick by the base and get it on.

So I moved my hips again, this time a bit deeper a dip and his head began to slip into me.

How he was hard in his sleep I don't know but I didn't care in the dark. I reached around him, brushing the covers off us, and gripped his lower back, keeping him in place. Leaning forward, I pushed back against him and he squelched quickly into me.

LAWD A GAAAD... that was it for me.

He woke up quick, fast and in a hurry and we only stopped about 30 minutes ago.

Remember I said that Andre is a demon? That boy is a DEMON!

I'd never had dick like this in my LIFE! I mean wow, it's a good looking penis first of all. Not too long, not too thick, it was like the third bowl of porridge. Just right. I've never been someone who took the time to appreciate a dick other than to use it for pleasure but I was mesmerised by it. Andre was humble and quite coy about it but it was a really sexy dick. And he knew exactly how to use that thing. For the first hour, he took his time just touching and kissing me. I know we were meant to be fucking but he was doing romantic kisses on the nape of my neck, brushing my hair and kissing across my shoulders.

Not the type of intimacy I'd been used to.

The second hour, replacement condoms and the lube came out.

The third hour, we were up against the floor-to-ceiling windows which were fully steamed with the cold condensation rubbing against my back.

The fourth hour was when I found my feet and flipped it on him and took control. Oh man, you should've seen me... I had that boy sweating like he stole something. He was a lot more muscular even though his frame appeared deceptively small, so it was beautiful to watch sex sweat drip off him.

Anything that we could balance on, sit on, lean on, stand against... whatever position that came to mind, we tried it.

By the fifth hour - yes the fifth hour - he was goading me to fuck his face. Orgasm-wise, I wasn't even counting but he had me cumming doing things that never worked before. He spoke to my pussy and I came. He didn't touch me, he just said things to her.

It was THE SHIT!

I honestly can't believe I'm up right now to be honest but I have to call work and tell them I'm not coming in.

What? Of course I'm not going in. I'm "sick" today. I've got a serious case of Vaginaius Mis Dickius and I need another day to get over it.

I mean shit, I can still feel the dick inside me right now and he's asleep.

I looked in the mirror and my blown out natural hair was all over the place. I looked like I'd been fucked. WELL!

I can't even put into words what happened but I'm glad the sink was there for me to lean on as a wave of something came over me and I shivered hungrily.

A quick pee and I was practising my best sick voice, ready to call work and tell them I wouldn't be coming in.

The phone rang and I hoped my manager wasn't in early and manning the phones. The receptionist answered.

My voice was husky and tired, an actual representation of how I felt at that moment. I gave my excuse and cut the phone off before she tried to engage in small talk. She was the type of woman who knew a home-made herbal remedy for everything.

Flushing the toilet, I brushed my hair away from my face and, looking in my own eyes, I could see flashbacks of the different ways I had an orgasm and the things I said in return. I like to consider myself quite a demure gentle woman with calm tones and eloquent language but I was sewer-mouthed last night.

Yeah, so you can see why I'm not going to work today. Before sleep slapped us both, we already talked about extending the length of stay by another day. He was in full agreement.

My wild mane calmed down as I brought my hands over my head to mat it down. I brushed my teeth and ran a flannel and shower gel over my edible and lickable bits and held the door handle ready to get back into bed.

I certainly wasn't ready to sleep and he was quite easy to raise in his sleep so he'd wake up eventually.

A heavy sigh sucked in and out of my chest and I shook my shoulders and opened the door, enjoying the saucy feeling that was exciting my mid-section.

Andre was already awake and staring at me with the covers pushed away and his legs open. For a second, it looked like three legs staring back at me and I did a double-take with a giggle.

'Sick yeah?' he said with a new bass in his voice that spoke directly to my vagina.

'What? Oh, you could hear me? Yeah, I'm not feeling well to be honest,' I chuckled with a hand on my chest followed by a very fake cough.

'OH NO!' he replied playfully then looked down at his dick. 'Is there anything I can do to make you feel better?'

The smile on my face was better than any words I could've followed up with. My eyes were dipping between his bearded cocaine-like smile and that dick that had me thinking about arranging another rendezvous.

The guy had talent!

I know I'm saying a lot about the dick but, if you're a woman and you've met a really beautiful penis then you know what I'm talking about.

Resting my hands on my hips and adjusting my weight to my left leg, I watched the hem of my nightie rise on my thigh.

'How about a snack before breakfast?'

He swung his legs off the bed and all three of them swung before me. 'I could definitely eat!'

Looking up at me, Andre called me with his index finger

and I walked towards him not taking my eyes away from his legs.

His hands slipped around my thighs, up to my waist and around to the small of my back. My right knee gave out and I buckled in his embrace. Securing me on my feet, he moved me back and kneeled in front of me while looking me in my face.

Embarrassment took over and I covered my face but he moved my hands and stared at me with solid, concentrated eyes. Those demanding, strong stares were killer as he delivered mean, deep long strokes earlier on.

A deep breath escaped my lungs and I tried to not look nervous as Andre's face dipped lower and lower. So low, all I could see were his eyes.

This was fun last night/ this morning in the throes of that sweet, that nasty, that gushy stuff but in the stone cold reality of the morning, my shyness returned.

His tongue lapped over both my lips and minty toothpaste-tinted breath rushed up at me.

'When did you...' was all I managed to say as his tongue straightened and he pushed forward until the tip touched my clit.

That was it for me as he spun around so my back was to the bed, arranged some pillows behind me and motioned for me to lay down but perched enough that I could still see what was going on.

Just before his face disappeared, he locked eyes with me and said three words that made me instantly wet.

'Breakfast in bed!'

OH MY DAAAAAAAAAAAAAAAAAAAAYS!

Sunday 4th February 2018

I've got dick on my mind!

It's Sunday, I'm home alone and refusing to move from my favourite corner on my sofa because every time I move, my body aches and groans from something Andre did to me the day before. I can't even eloquently put into words what he did to me but it was amazing. You know that Az Yet song *Last Night*? I've never understood their idea of sex where you see the sun, the stars, the moon and heaven but I damn sure do now. I saw black spots, bright spots, flashes of light and at one point I wasn't sure which way was up. That was when I was running from him because he'd been eating my pussy for 38 minutes. No breaks, no stops for orgasms... just straight 38 minutes. And when I did come, he'd eat me some more.

The FUCK!?!

I think that was when I blacked out.

Now I'm at home curled up in a gentle foetal position paying no attention to Big Shaq's *Man's Not Hot* video which always made me smile.

If I'm honest, I had shit to do. Lots of shit. Because I was "sick" yesterday and didn't go into work, I forgot about a very important meeting I was meant to attend. A meeting I was running. Luckily, the meeting was cancelled but that didn't mean my manager wasn't going to call me via Skype. He text me and told me earlier this morning.

It's not my fault I forgot, we all know who is to blame. Andre.

I've been laying with my head on a cushion like I lost my

favourite pet. I must've looked morose and miserable but I was lost in a scene-by-scene flashback of the moment I woke up and slipped him in for the first time. And no, we are NOT gonna talk about the fact that I fucked him without a condom. It was just a little bit. Mind your own business! Some of you reading this right now have made some sketchy decisions for a bit of pleasure so glass stones and homes alright?

I'm literally mind fucking myself because it's the little things like remembering how he ran his hands up my legs, feeling it all over again and giggling like an idiot. But he's not even here.

When I got home from the hotel, I gave the girls the full tea with dirty receipts and you should've seen the things they said.

$imone: Hey ladies...

Russia: Oh wow, so you finally came up for air did ya?

Kat: Nuh uhhh, you can't come in here with a simple "hey ladies". You need to talk and now!

B: Yeah sis, you've not even answered to me. Are you okay?

Russia: You walking funny?

$imone: I'm curled up on the sofa in a ball and I'm not moving.

Kat: I KNEW IT! I KNEW IT! So what was it like? Was it big, small but worked? Any foreplay?

Russia: I wanna know if he went down on you.

Kat: Ooo yaas, fuck all my questions, answer that one. Did he eat you like ice cream or was it like licking a lemon?

$imone: Trina, you are fucking nuts you know that. And

for the record, he ate me like a black man with a well-seasoned, succulent and full-bodied piece of fresh off the barbecue chicken… yes he did! Sucked the marrow…

My phone continued to blow up with messages after that and I entertained my girls with every single detail I could recollect. As much as I told them I couldn't remember how many times I came, I knew it was in the high 30s. If I combined every orgasm I had from foreplay, oral, actual sex and that thing where he spoke to my pussy… yeah, high 30s, low 40s. I'd actually lost count but I was only working in estimates.

I told them about the sex all over the room and Katrina began quoting lyrics from Skepta's *All Over The House*.

And she wasn't wrong. The way Andre wielded his dick around that hotel room like a lightsabre was at times awe-inspiring. In between position changes and moments where I just needed to breath, Andre looked at me in this… way. It was like hunger mixed with ego and anticipation. All the while holding his dick in the palm of his hand, just waiting for me to be ready.

I didn't tell them that we had sex without a condom as I just didn't want to have to deal with the drama. My sister would have the most to say, Russia would be second and Katrina would have the least to say. Mainly because Russia and Katrina had raw moments with some of their random sex partners in the past so they couldn't talk.

I'd been checking Andre's What's App since I woke up and he had not checked the last good morning message I sent him so he must've still been asleep.

While *Hollyoaks* played mindlessly in the background, my

laptop screeched the Skype ringtone and I could see it was time for the conversation with my manager. Brushing myself down and putting a wooly hat over my bushy hair, I answered the voice call.

'Morning Simone,' Faizon said cheerfully.

'Morning...' I replied tiredly.

'So... who's the dick?'

My face screwed up in confusion and comedy and I was glad this was just a voice call so he couldn't see me holding my hands over my mouth.

'Who is the WHAT?'

'The dick! You've not taken a day off since you started this job. You've worked through flu, infections, period pains and anything else you women take days off work for. Then one day Simone is sick? It's gotta be dick!'

Faizon is gay, so his ability to be overly brash in a work environment took some getting used to. This line of questioning was not out of character for him.

'No, I was really sick. I think it was food poisoning.'

'Must've been some good dick to make you miss YOUR OWN meeting yesterday.'

During the slaying of my pussy yesterday, I did stop for a minute and think about work. I had a 'what would I be doing at work right now' thought but the meeting didn't creep in there either.

'Yeah, it must've been a 24-hour thing because I'm okay now. I've been looking through the storyboard and I wanna make sure we capture the crash just perfectly. I know we don't have access to London Bridge like that but imagine what we could...'

'Does this dick have a name?'

'Oh my God Faizon, focus man!'

'Was it one of those like perfect dicks with the veins and the length and a little bit of girth?'

'No, no and no.'

But he wasn't far off!

Andre had something I'd never seen before: a perfect penis.

It was... I swear... Like perfect in every way. It had the tiniest hook to it too. Like a curve up so it touched walls and went up a little bit, which, if you know, then you know why it's a perfect dick.

'Have you got any pictures of it?'

'Fazion!? So we got the interview with the security guards and I'm still waiting to see if we can get a Russell Reed interview to put a cherry on everything.'

'I didn't call to talk about work shit, I wanna hear about this dick!'

'Have we heard from Channel 4?'

'They want to speak to YOU. They're gonna have an exec call you today, I gave them your Skype info. Come on at least give me inches!?'

I rolled my eyes and began talking bad connection in between random mutes.

'So... I've...my cousin... to help... locations for... titles... send e-mail....'

Then I cut the call.

Faizon was an excellent manager and was usually very focussed but when it came to sex, his promiscuous ways always came to the front and he wanted details, sizes and vein definitions.

The thing was I wanted to talk about it. I wanted to talk about Andre and everything my body was going through and it was more than 12 hours since he touched me. That meant fuck all because I could still feel the moment we both looked down at his dick and watched as he slipped the whole thing into me. That made my eyes roll back just a little... I think I scratched him once or twice.

I honestly wasn't ready for it all so it was kind of an emotion overload.

Checking his What's App every few minutes with still two black ticks, I lay back down and got lost in a daydream of our time in the shower.

'Hmmm.... fucking hell...' I said in frustration.

My phone beeped and I checked my What's App.

It was a message from Andre.

Because it's only me talking to you, I can tell you straight up, I was excited as fuck! I know I'd only seen him yesterday but I missed him. I wasn't someone who had a stable of fuck buddies and friends with benefits. If I wasn't in a relationship then I didn't do sex with random people. I just didn't flex that way. Well there was that one time with that guy Marcus but that just confirmed why I didn't do it. Too much drama.

But Andre didn't just fuck me. Well, he DID, but he didn't just buss and then straight getting dressed. He laid there with me afterwards and just breathed with me. After a flurry of orgasms, with me on top, he'd stay inside me and hold my head against his chest and just hold me. I mean, he'd spank me something rotten and then massage the place he'd just spanked. That's after-care ladies. Not every man who spanks knows about after-care.

I opened his chat conversation and waited for him to say something.

Andr3: Good morning miss sunshine. I can't lie, I've been thinking about you since I woke up this morning. I honestly can't let 24-hours pass without either tasting you or being inside you. Please let me know what you are doing today and let's see what we can work out.

My fingers were so excited, I dropped my phone and felt my heart beat racing. I looked down at my clothes, thinking about what I had clean to change into. I asked him to call me while springing off the sofa, looking for something to wear that would denote my chilling at home but also be a lil' sexy and clean.

My phone rang and I did an air bicycle of excitement with my feet before answering the phone.

'What's up buff stuff?' he said with energy.

'You alright Andre?' I offered back, holding in my urge to invite him round straight away.

'Is there any time in this day where I can finish eating your pu...'

'Where are you?'

'I'm in Stratford, I've just finished doing some last-minute shopping before my business trip and I really can't get you out of my head.'

'You're about 15 minutes away. I'll send you my address and you can come round.'

'You sure Miss Simone? That means that I'll be in your house. This is only like day three or four and...'

'Are you judging me Andre?'

He laughed.

I messaged him my address and postcode while pulling out a bodysuit and tracksuit bottoms which cinched at the waist and made my body look explosive from the hips down.

'I've sent it. So, does that mean I'm gonna see you soon?'

'I'm already on my way.'

'Okay see you soon,' I said calmly, threw in a mumbled goodbye and threw my phone on my bed and hit the bathroom. I had a flash shower and was in my bodysuit and tracksuit bottoms ready in minutes. I'd pulled my hair down and competed two thick plaits which ran down my shoulders.

According to my wall clock, I'd only taken six minutes so I began to clean, which was pointless because my space is spotless. Clean home, clean mind and all that so I just sat back in my spot on the sofa and waited.

I spared a thought for the fact that Andre was about to be in my private space which only 30% of boyfriends of the past got to see.

I'm very private about my home because it's just that: my home! My style is cultural and minimal so lots of bare walls but Ankhra material on my sofa. Very Valerie McKenzie.

I checked the time, picturing where he was between Stratford and my place. If my maths was correct, he would be arriving in the next five minutes and my sweaty armpits told me I was ready.

A message came through on my phone and I screamed in excitement.

DO NOT TELL MY GIRLS THAT I SCREAMED!

'Ooooo, he's downstairs,' I said to myself excitedly.

Kicking my M&Ms cover off my feet and folding it over the edge of the sofa, I told him what to press on the outside door and stood behind my front door.

Although my body still ached and creamed due to his previous day's work, I still wanted more of what Andre could do. Just the idea of having even two orgasms had me running excitedly on the spot.

On the other side of my front door, I could hear the lift opening to my floor. I looked myself up and down, smelled my armpits, rubbed cocoa butter-flavoured Vaseline on my lips and smoothed my eyebrows.

Through my peep-hole, I watched Andre walking and checking door numbers, creeping closer. I felt something run down and tickle the inside of my leg.

'Come to me penis...' I whispered behind the door.

Andre turned and inspected my deep blue door, looking at my flap and doorbell. As he moved to press the bell, I opened the door slightly, moving behind it at the same time.

'Simone?' he said to the open the door.

'Yeah, come on in,' I peeked round the door with a smile and he smiled back.

'I had a daydream that I walked into the wrong place and suddenly there's an e-fit description of me on the news saying I'm armed and dangerous.'

Just the air of him walking past me had me dripping down my other leg and I rubbed my thighs together to remove the tickling feeling.

In my head, I'm talking to myself about how insane it is that I'm wet and he hasn't even touched me yet. That has never happened before.

Closing the door softly, I turned around and Andre was already in my space. He exhaled and minty air escaped from his lips that I was already staring at.

His arms snuck around my waist and he pulled me closer.

'Nice place you got here.'

My arms locked around his neck. 'You haven't seen anything yet. We're just standing in the corridor.'

He waited for me to stop talking before he smiled and kissed me.

Taking me by surprise, he pressed his body against mine and gave me... it was like a movie kiss.

I don't know if my leg kicked up but I felt it.

'I'm talking about this place,' Andre said, grabbing a handful of my left bum cheek.

'Well, let me give you the tour.'

My laptop interrupted our sexy lyric moment as a Skype ringtone chirped from my living room.

I had to unwrap myself from Andre's embrace and run before it cut off. Remembering Faizon telling me that someone from Channel 4 would be calling, I had to get my head into work mode.

'Gimme a second, I just have to take a call from work and then we can....'

'Don't worry,' he said following behind me. 'Do your thing. I'm here when you're ready.'

I connected headphones and clicked the mouse to answer the call.

'Hello? Yes this is she... hiiiiiiii.'

The executive introduced himself as Colin and I could instantly picture a middle-aged white man with a Peter Griffin belly and thinning hair on top just from the sound of his voice. His moving image came through on the screen.

Though my voice and demeanour was in work-mode, my body wanted Andre. I looked over to him on my single seater chair and he was already looking at me. In fact, he was standing up and was pulling a t-shirt over his head.

I mouthed: what the fuck are you doing?

He replied by stepping out of his tan shoes and began to unbuckle his belt.

A question from chubby-exec grabbed my attention and I was back in work-mode.

I could feel Andre moving towards me and I looked up just as his groin flashed past my face. I brought my laptop to my chest so the rest of the room couldn't be seen.

He watched me talk as he put his hands on my waistband and shuffled them down my thighs. I shook my head but I wanted to see where this was going to go. Holding a professional tone in my voice while watching my tracksuit bottoms come off one leg at a time, I grinned my sexiest grin.

'Well I think it's an important story to be told because Tatiana Blue is a hero to most. She's an example of someone who decided to take her life into her own hands and get what she... felt she was owed. Of course she did that via a life of crime but in this country there's a weird appreciation for criminals. Look at the Krays. Do you know how many documentaries and films I've seen about the Krays? And what are they famous for? Gangs, violence, murder... but they loved their mother and cared about the community right? How... how... HOW is Tatiana Blue any different? She wasn't violent without cause, I've got interviews with 60 different security guards who've met her and can attest to that. She gave back to the community with her "drops" and she single-handedly improved not only the confidence of the bigger woman... but she was the unofficial spokesperson for US.'

The pauses in my speech were because Andre took of my tracksuit bottoms, spread my thighs and started eating my pussy while I could do nothing but watch.

The exec asked me for more information but Andre began fucking me with his tongue. 'Can I call you back in a minute? I'm just... FUUUUUUUCK!'

Monday 5th February 2018

Welcome to monthly girls night!

It's my turn to host so the girls have descended onto my humble abode for *Call Of Duty*, trash eating, memes and random videos on Youtube and hilarious conversation, all sponsored by a sweet amount of alcohol.

We did this once a month and used it as an opportunity to catch-up on loose gossip from the previous month as well as an amazing cheat day. It was okay because we were each other's gym buddies so we supported the massive takeaway session. I ordered the Chinese, Russia always wanted Indian and Brina and Katrina didn't care, they just wanted food.

The kitchen usually ended up being the hub of our meetings because one of us would get up for food, someone else would follow and start talking and before you knew it, we were all in the kitchen standing up and having a conversation.

Armed with my plate of Singapore noodles, a spoon of chicken Korma and shredded chilli beef with a few prawn balls and chicken wings on the edge of my plate, I shuffled in my *Adventure Time* slippers and took my position in the corner of my sofa.

Knowing how I kept my home, the girls brought their own slippers so they didn't drag their shoes on my floors and they all walked into the living room with their food on trays. Katrina had music television on and Giggs was on the screen being his cool, smooth self.

I like Giggs.

Before you ask, yes, my phone was hot because of all the messages Andre had been sending me. And I sat down with my food checking the last message he sent, which was a picture of his dick in a beautiful light.

I actually zoned out of the room and was taken back 24-hours to the moment Andre had me bent over the sofa holding my cheeks open and slow-stroking me through the most intense, brutal, stomach-gripping orgasms I'd ever had.

OOOOO, that was rough!

And that's the thing about Andre's penis. It is a feat of magic, a marvel, a thing of beauty that was a joy forever, it was just swell. You know some dicks just go in and out and you have to find a way to make it work for you. Not this dick... oh no... this dick came with instant gratification. From the moment Andre had my tracksuit bottoms on the floor and had popped the buttons on my bodysuit, I was already on the edge of an orgasm. And that was just in anticipation of what he was going to do to me. And of course he did it. Lost count YET AGAIN of how many orgasms he made me have spread across the same sofa my girls were sitting on with plates of food.

There must've been a stupid smile on my face because

my sister was the first to say something.

'Sim got a dick piiiiiiiiiiiic!' Brina shouted to the other girls. I was so engrossed in the picture that I didn't see or feel her leaning to look at my phone.

'Lemme see,' Russia said, damn near dropping her plate.

'Oooo where?' Katrina said with a chicken wing hanging out of her mouth.

I turned my phone and showed it to them as a ripple of excitement started at the base of my spine and travelled all the way up.

My girls huddled around my phone. I watched their eyes looking up and down at the picture of Andre holding his dick in his hand. It sat pretty big in his palm.

'No wonder you sitting on the ting as much as you can. Is it good? Tell the truth.'

I locked my phone and sat back under a spoonful of noodles and beef thinking about the answer to that question. I'd not been shy in telling them how good it was but I could tell that Katrina was asking me a deeper question.

'It's a damn good dick and its attached to a fine man. That's all I'm going to say.'

'It's got a hook to it,' she said. 'Does it reach the... you know the... promised land?'

My eyes must've said everything because Katrina burst into her high-pitched laughter with her feet running on the spot quickly. And then I had no control over what came out of my mouth next.

'You know how Ulysses Klaue describes Wakanda in *Black Panther*? Like a secret that no-one knows about but it's there in plain sight? That's the way I think about this dick! It is like a cheat day with steak, chips and peanut butter and banana milkshake afterwards and finished with pecan pie with *Baileys* cream and a high grade spliff for dessert. His dick is Wakanda!'

'Whoa,' Russia replied wide-eyed.

'Damn sis, he's got it like that?'

'Does it slip out and he's able to slip it back in without using his hand?'

'Yep!'

'That boy has dick control ladies and ladies! Can we raise our drinks for good dick control?'

We all raised our glasses and laughed as Russia went into a story about her last encounter with good dick control. Meanwhile, my phone, which I switched to vibrate, was rumbling next to my thigh. I knew it was Andre, probably saying something which would entice me and send me into a world of flashbacks and phantom strokes which made my legs clamp together.

'Can I see that picture again? Better yet, send it to me,' Katrina said.

'Like you haven't got dick pics in your phone. I've seen them… you've got a United Colours of Benneton folder of dick pics in your phone right now.'

'Why you chatting my business? NO more folder time for you!'

The girls laughed together around a table of pineapple Ciroc, Captain Morgan's Spice Rum, two bottles of Baileys and half empty bottles of wine.

I was doing damage to my plate while my vibrating phone was distracting me immensely. I wanted to read what Andre was sending me. I wanted to read in private so I could gush and giggle and wriggle around as his words worked their magic on me.

The urge took over and I picked up my phone.

Andre:

Are you sitting on your sofa?

Are you sitting on the exact spot where you begged me to stop fucking you?

You know I haven't stopped thinking about you.

You see the way you kiss me? There's cocaine in your kiss!

There's something about the way you cum... It's like an event and I love it.

How's girls night going? Have they asked about me?

Have you told them about the "nines"? Did you get the wet patch out?

I swear, I just need a taste. Honestly, I just want to be inside you right now.

Simone, you are killing me right now, what are you doing to me?

What if I told you I'm gonna be passing your place in about 15 minutes?

You could leave your front door open and I could sneak in the bathroom.

Fucking hell Simone... I can't concentrate.

Well it's good to see I wasn't the only one suffering over here. I was there in the room with my girls but mentally and spiritually, I was on top of Andre with my hands above my head. And that's deep for me. I've got a roll or two on my stomach and I absolutely fucking hate them. And I can't shift them either. I do sit-ups, every stomach exercise you can imagine, I've done it. I've bought all those bollocks things on the late-night commercials that promise abs-while-you-work and they've done fuck all. When it comes to sexy time, I'll always find a way to cover my rolls with a t-shirt, scarf or just covering them with my hands. I did that at the hotel and Andre moved my hands and replaced them with his own.

Ladies, that man rubbed my stomach in a way that made the hair on the back of my neck stand up. He's got BIG hands so his palms spread over my whole stomach. By the time he came round yesterday, I felt comfy enough to get on top and ride him freely with my hands in the air. And believe me they were waving like I just didn't care.

That level of comfort was strange so quickly but with the added bonus of the curved dick touching my G-Spot, it was all good with me.

I looked at the door to the living room and thought about how easy or difficult it would be to sneak Andre in for a very quick, very rampant moment in the bathroom. The scene from *Soul Food* crept into my head and I smiled into my last prawn ball.

'That's a dick smile if ever I've seen one,' my sister said, looking at me with knowing eyes.

'So what do we think ladies? Early stages?' Russia said, pouring a glass of Ciroc and ginger beer.

'I dunno… she's been giving us the details and he sounds like he's got the power but she's still calm so I don't know.'

'But sometimes the calm ones are calm until…'

'Oh yeah until…'

'That until is brutal!'

I was lost. My head was flicking between them all, having no idea what they were talking about.

'Ladies, what in the fuck are you talking about?'

Katrina took the floor. 'We are trying to ascertain if you, my dear friend, are in the early stages of what is eloquently called dick addiction.'

'Yes Miss Simone. It has been three days and you've seen him twice correct?'

'Well actually…'

Every set of eyes was now focussed on me at the prospect of something exciting coming out of my mouth.

'Actually?' my sister was on the edge of her seat.

'I saw him yesterday as well.'

Six eyes all widened at me and I could see the different questions they had ready to shoot. I attempted to cut them off before they fired.

'He came round yesterday, yes it was the absolute shit and I can officially say that I have broken in my place. Every single room.'

Katrina screamed and stomped her feet, giving Russia a

high five as she clinked glasses with my sister.

The follow-up questions followed at the same time.

'Wait, he came HERE to your yard?' That was from my sister.

'How many times did he make you cum? This could be the decider for the prognosis of dick addiction?' That was Russia.

'When you say every single room, you mean the living room too? I'm a freak so I know how to fuck in a living room and I know you lot fucked on this sofa that I'm sitting on right now.'

I looked at where Katrina was sitting and the flashback was instantaneous. On the last cushion on the edge of the sofa was where Andre had me laying flat on my stomach and, with his feet on the ground, was leaning over me sliding the sweetest of consistent strokes in me. I blacked out at one point but I don't think he noticed.

The length of my silence and probably the dirty smile on my face told Katrina everything and she jumped up with a yelp.

'Don't worry, I cleaned afterwards.'

'Listen, we need to look at the biggest thing in this story. She had him HERE girls. He's been in the yard. And you know how private Miss Simone is!?'

Russia and Katrina made large O's with their mouths.

Meanwhile, my phone was vibrating like crazy again and I wanted another fix of his words.

'Sim never has man at her place!' Russia laughed. 'This changes everything. This might be beyond early stages ladies.'

'Can you lot stop talking about me like I'm not here?'

'You're not here,' Katrina added. 'The dick's got you now. And it looks like you don't even know it yet, which is a dangerous time.'

'Ah because she hasn't had the until yet.'

'The fuck is the until?'

It was Russia's turn to take the podium. She brushed her dreadlocks which ran down to her lower back and cleared her throat.

'The until is the moment when you are getting regular dick and it's all good UNTIL it stops and you are sent into a world of instant cold turkey and you don't know what to do with yourself. This is a dangerous time because you are capable of doing anything at that point. You might do something stupid and try and recreate the magic with some random dick and it just won't do it for you. Which will piss you off even more. You're decision-making capabilities may not be as strong as they were because of this dick. Then you might get a bit stalkerish when you try and contact that dick and it doesn't respond. Now you start internalising. Now you start asking yourself "what is wrong with me? Why isn't he calling me back?" And by that point, you are well and truly dickmatised and the only way to quell that hunger is to get some of that same dick. The same dick that got you here in the first place. So now you're stuck in a vicious cycle that you can't get out of because the dick is too good to leave alone. And not only can't you leave it alone, you also have the realisation that you may never get dick THIS good again. This dick stays on your mind. It never leaves. Even while you are doing random, non-sexual things, the dick pops into your head like an afterthought. You may even ask yourself why did you start fucking with the dick... and at the same time wonder when you're gonna see it again. This is the dick that worries us, that hooks and traps us. This dick causes more problems than it solves... but you don't care because you are having the best sex of your entire sexual career. For this type of dick you must beware because it doesn't just caress your walls and reach for your stomach. It touches your mind... it grooves in your soul and it'll make you offer him a spare key so the dick can be waiting for you when you get home, right Katrina? And yes this is coming from experience... beware of that D! It will drive you absolutely crazy.'

Brina and Katrina raised their hands and clicked in Russia's direction while I laughed hysterically. I'd heard of the term 'dickmatised' but I'd never subscribed to the notion because it had never happened to me. Not that I knew of.

This wasn't that... I was just getting some good-good and it was good, plain and simple.

I shrugged. 'Thanks for the advice and that absolutely epic dissertation but I'm good. No dick addiction here.'

'Tut tut tut,' Brina giggled. 'It's sad when they have no idea.'

Gathering all the plates, I went to the kitchen, making sure to have my phone with me. Leaving them on the side, instead of putting them straight in the dishwasher like I always do, I was straight into my phone.

Andre:

So, I'm about five minutes away... How possible would it be to see you?

You could leave the door on the latch, close the living room door...

I could message you to say I'm here then you could need the "toilet".

How naughty are you feeling right now?

I know what this is and what we are but is it okay to say I miss you?

We could have a moment like in *Soul Food*. Have you seen that film?

Sorry, I'm not tryin to encroach on your evening... I just... ya know...

Tell me you're not wet just thinking about it?

I'm outside your building right now!

HOLY FUCKING SHIT HE WAS SERIOUS!

There was no way I was ready to believe him until he sent a picture of himself standing outside my block with a sexy yet sinister smile on his face. I'd seen that smile up close and it was usually accompanied by a move or something that would make me cum unexpectedly.

For a moment, I felt trapped in my kitchen. I looked out the window trying to see him but my view was obstructed by buildings. To get to my intercom, I'd have to walk past my girls who were already watching me. But I was dying to find out if he was telling the truth.

I wrote a message, ready to call his bluff.

$imone: If you're really outside press my buzzer then!

I sent the message. I watched the moment he received the message with two blue ticks. I saw him go from online to nothing. Looking up, waiting for the sound of my intercom, I smiled but was tense at the same time.

After a few seconds of silence, I laughed to myself, got a larger glass for an even larger drink and went back to my spot on the sofa.

I spied Katrina looking at me.

'What?'

'Just watching for the signs that's all.'

'There is NO dick addic...'

My intercom buzzed and made us all jump. My heart was on instant sprint and I jumped up quicker than everyone else.

'Who the fuck is that?' I said, trying to hide my fear and excitement. 'Sis, did you order any more food?'

'No, maybe it's someone trying to get into the building.'

Once I left the room, I closed the door behind me, sending my corridor into complete darkness. I manoeuvred my hallway in the dark and answered my intercom phone.

'Hello?' My palm was sweating, my front face cheeks were hurting from smiling and I crossed my legs and danced my toes on the floor.

'Oh you thought I was playing?!'

SWEET JESUS, MARY, JOSEPH AND NOAH… this fucking guy was outside my place. I'd like to act all cool, calm and collected but an excited energy surged through me just at the sound of his voice. I could feel it creeping across my skin like silk and I neede… I mean wanted it in my ear.

'No well… yeah but…'

'So what you do now is…' he said with a commanding air in his voice. 'You turn off the sound on your intercom, buzz me in, leave your door on the latch then go back to the girls and say it was a wrong number or a wrong door.'

'Oh is that what I do?' I whispered in the dark.

'You can do what you want miss Simone. If the idea isn't interesting you, I can go about my business and we can arrange something for another time. I just… want to be inside you just for a moment.'

'For fuck sake, you can't say those type of things and not…'

'So buzz me in and I'll do the rest.'

I moved the phone from my ear and looked up, stuck on what to do. There were so many things I was thinking that could go wrong but, at the same time, I wanted him inside me.

The *Soul Food* scene came into my head again. You know Bird and Lem in the bathroom scene?

If you've seen that film then you know what I'm talking about.

I cleared my throat.

'NO, THERE ISN'T A CHRISTIAN HERE… YOU'VE GOT THE WRONG PLACE MY FRIEND!'

I turned the volume down and pressed the entry button before hanging up. Pressing my body against the door, I unlocked it and left it on the latch before taking giddy steps back to the living room.

'I don't know why people think they can use me to get into different apartments. Does my door number look like reception?' I moaned to no-one particular.

Slamming the living room door, I jumped back into my spot, listening to everything. I wanted to see if I could hear the door open or his footsteps. I honestly couldn't believe I was doing this to be honest and I put my thumbnail in my mouth and began to tap my teeth. The girls were talking about a question posed by sex advice/all-round saucepot @Oloni on Twitter and were taking no notice of me as I finally got to pour my large drink.

I heard a door slam and perked up like a meerkat sensing danger. Luckily no-one clocked but I caught myself and sat back in my corner. I was trying to focus my hearing but there were too many colours from a music video, sounds and meme videos from everyone's phones. Something made my shoulders shrug and it sounded like my front door closing quietly. My eyes shot to the wall, imagining I could look through to see if Andre was in or not. My heart was racing on a different speed. My legs were up against my chest and I was spinning my phone between my fingers.

A large sip of my extremely fiery drink, which was a mix of rum and Ciroc and rose wine I think, and I was excited! My eyes and ears were trying to pay attention but were losing to the live, loud pulse of the room. Katrina sparked a spiff even though I always tell her to take it outside. I already know she's gonna tell me it's too cold to go outside. I pulled out an ashtray from under my centre table and slid it to her.

My phone vibrates.

'So Oloni asks: do you ever feel disgusted with yourself after you masturbate and watch porn? What say thee ladies?' Russia looked up at us and took the spliff from Katrina.

'That depends on what kind of orgasm I have and the reason I'm knocking one out. If it's because I'm just horny and need a release then cool but if that prick face isn't giving me any and I have to get myself off then I feel shitty afterwards.'

'Is there a divorce anywhere in your near future sis?' I asked.

'You KNOW it's complicated.'

'Complicated how? He cheats, you know and yet you guys are still together.'

'Do YOU ever feel embarrassed when you masturbate Simone?'

I knew it was time for a subject change when my sister said my name in that way. She didn't like talking about Donovan, her husband.

My phone vibrated in my lap and I tried to not react. My body, on the other hand, came to life. My nipples perked, my toes wiggled, my stomach dipped and I knew I was wet. It could've been any notification but any and every notification belonged to Andre. Or at least it better had.

Brina stood up suddenly and stretched before walking to the living room door. She did it so casually, I wasn't ready because I was checking a message from Andre which said he was inside and waiting for me in the bathroom.

I looked up from the message to see Brina closing the door behind her.

'Wait, hold o… shiiiiiiiiit…'

My fingers got to work typing a super quick message so Andre didn't think my sister was me. I'd managed to get the message sent before she got to the bathroom. Delivered and I heard the door close.

I looked to the left and the right while Russia and Katrina were laughing at the ImJusbait app. I was waiting for an almighty scream to erupt from the bathroom and my sister to run out screaming about the black man in my bathroom. But there were no screams, no shouts of help, nothing. The toilet flushed and my taps ran for a moment. Still no loud voices, no hail Mary screams, nothing. The door closed and the living room door opened and my sister stared me straight in the face.

'What you looking at?' she said, freezing on the spot.

'How was your pee? Did you enjoy yourself?'

'What kind of weird fucking question is that? Did I enjoy my pee!? Who the fuck asks that question?'

'No need to be rude, geez. Anyway, I need a number two. Back in a day or two.'

'That is just nasty!' Katrina mumbled without looking up from her phone.

Rushing past my sister, I heard her say: 'who the hell is so excited to take a shit?'

But I was!

I closed the living room door, sprang two steps to the bathroom and opened and closed it. Locked it too. The room was pitch black and the light switch was on the outside. I went to reach for it and a strong hand clamped around my wrist. Another hand snuck up my back, around my shoulder and neck.

My tap opened there and then and I purred.

'Well hello you...' Andre said in a low deep gruff next to my ear.

'YOU, sir, are a piece of freaking trouble in my life.'

''A good problem?'

'MY problem!'

His body pressed against mine and I bumped into the door. His hand on my neck was something I didn't know I liked but I sure did need it. His other hand circled my stomach and squeezed it and that's when I fell back into him.

'Where did you hide when my...'

Andre didn't let me finish the sentence because he bent me over the sink, pulled my tracksuit bottoms down and I could hear the jingle of his belt buckle. I held the sink squarely and assumed a strong position bent at the waist. Reaching back in the dark, I felt for his dick, which was hard and leaking at the head. With the tip of my thumb, I rubbed the liquid over his dick and smushed him between my wet lips.

Holding him in place, he pushed with his hips and slid inside me and I gasped loudly. He put his hand over my mouth and slipped all the way into me and I slapped the sink. Flushing the toilet with my foot, I felt Andre spread my cheeks while my girls laughed together from the living room.

Tuesday 6th February 2018

There is never a better gym session than a gym session with dick on the brain. I was pushing myself on everything: extra minutes on the treadmill, extra reps on each machine and double the laps in the swimming pool. Work was another long day filled with a lot of talking now that Channel 4 wanted to be involved in our Tatiana Blue documentary. They were happy in general but wanted to make a few changes that my bosses were happy to oblige with.

I was happy with anything because my mind wasn't fully on the job. It was somewhere else getting fucked in the dark with a hand over my mouth. Moaning all muffled and shit. Full blown humping the shit out of me.

Didn't help that Andre was on the end of his phone today so as soon as I'd send him something, he'd reply almost instantly. This was not helped further by the random dick pics he sent in between the conversation. I don't know if he knew what he was doing to me but I didn't care. I just liked seeing the dick.

Oh, I've stopped counting orgasms by the way because there's just no point. Even in the bathroom, the moment he slipped in, I came. By the time he covered my mouth, I came again. We were in there for about five maybe six minutes.

It's really all about the maths!

Wiping my face with my towel, I checked my phone and saw laughing emojis. I'd already sent a request to see him after the gym to which he'd agreed, saying he was going to suggest the same thing.

Great minds and groins think alike apparently.

Finishing my session, I packed my things with the quickness and got home in record time. My shower was amazing, singing off-key like *I wiiiiiish I never met her at all!* My Victoria Secret outfits were delivered by the building concierge after my shower and I tried them on, choosing which one I wanted Andre to rip off me. Well not rip because these things cost money but if he wanted to tear it a little bit, I'd let him.

Checking my phone, Andre said he was leaving work and was about to be on his way. I plaited my hair in two cane-rolls, donned my pink teddy with silk dressing gown and my Charlotte Olympia shoes, courtesy of one of Tatiana Blue's infamous, legendary "drops".

Ladies, let me tell you I am ready for the dick. Yes I am.

I took the shoes off and walked to the kitchen, preparing a bottle of wine and two glasses. I lit candles around the living room, put on my slow jam playlist and burned a Black Love incense stick.

Took a moment to look around.

NOW I'm ready!

My reflection greeted me in my full-length mirror and I stared at myself.

'Is that how you're going on yeah? Look at yooooou though. Listen, tonight we are taking this dick on a journey, you hear me?'

Sucking in my stomach, I stuck one leg forward - Instagram-pose style - and visualised all the places where Andre would be kissing me. The way he would peel my clothes off me like they were bubble wrap protecting a precious artefact. The trail he would lead over each inch of my skin with his lips before his dick came anywhere near me. The eyes he'd give me as he licked my lips, making them nice and wet before sliding his tongue inside me. That last one he liked to do a lot. Which is strange for me because any man that's given me head has always done it with the lights off. Every time. Sure, some of them have been guys who say they don't so they want the lights off to hide the "shame" but even those who were open to a little snack wanted the lights off too. But Andre liked to watch. He liked the whole damn show and he liked to hear me tell him when I'm cumming. I've always been a quiet nutter, lol. But this guy has me screaming out his name, my name, the Lord's name. One time, and I'm not joking, I screamed out *ASHER D AND I'M THE STAR OF THE SHOW!*

No joke! I had to explain afterwards about my crush on Ashley Walters and my So Solid addiction circa '98-'01.

My phone vibrated and it was a message from Andre which made my shoulder shimmy. 'Yeah bring that penis here boy!'

YOU FUCKING WHAT?!?!?!?

I didn't look at the message properly but all I saw was the apology and the words, 'we're gonna have to rearrange...' and 'work emergency'. My smile dropped almost instantly and my shoulders dropped afterwards.

Falling back on my sofa, I looked around and I swear on my job, I felt like I wanted to cry. Looking around at the candles, which were giving a sweet ass mood lighting, the music, the glasses and the wine, my wickedly sexy outfit which felt ridiculous and over the top now... EURRRRGH!

'OH FOR FUCK SAKE!' I yelled while stamping my feet up and down.

I went back to my phone and stared at the message again, just to make sure I didn't read it wrong. How can he cancel? I mean... we arranged it.

Andr3: Simone the queen of the hierarchy, I'm so sorry but I'm gonna have to cancel tonight. I've been called back to work... they've called everyone in for some kind of work emergency. Sorry for the short notice. I'll call you later.

This was a moment when I wished my eyes lied to me. Leaning back on the sofa, damn near lying down, I crossed my leg and suddenly felt extremely naked. I draped the see-through dressing gown over my leg and suddenly I wanted to be out of this outfit.

I was huffing and puffing with my thoughts running though all the things that could possibly happen at his work for the WHOLE staff team to be called in.

Then I stopped and asked myself, 'What does Andre DO?'

Scanning through our conversations from my mental roladex, I couldn't remember a moment where he told me what he did for a living. My eyebrows screwed up and I rushed my thumbs to our conversations and looked for a job convo but I couldn't find anything.

My mind coupled those thoughts with the fact that Andre said he didn't have any social media. No Facebook, no Instgram, no Twitter, SnapChat or Tumblr. And for some reason, that was strange to me. EVERYONE was on something or other. If he had What's App, he would at least have a Facebook account. But my random searches for his name came up empty.

Yes, of COURSE I went looking for him. I searched every social media app I had for him and came up with nothing. Curiosity got the better of me after the first night in the hotel and I got my Agent Gibbs on. (Yeah, *NCIS* is my shit!)

Meanwhile, here I am, looking like a tramp at the Bunny

Ranch with no lips on my shoulders, no fingers rubbing my clit, no dick slow stroking me to some of the most explosive orgasms I've ever had.

'FOR FUCKS SAKE!' I screamed again and jumped to my feet.

Anger. That's what is coursing through me right now.

Still couldn't think of a reason why the entire work force would get called into work at...

'9pm!?'

My phone vibrated again and I brought it up so quickly I almost hit myself in the face.

It was the girl's group. Katrina and Russia were wishing me a happy dick night. Which proceeded to annoy me that little bit more.

'I haven't even replied to the guy,' I reminded myself.

My fingers typed my instant thought.

$imone: FOR FUCK SAKE ANDRE... DO YOU KNOW WHAT I DID FOR YOU TONIGHT? DO YOU KNOW HOW SEXY I FUCKING LOOK RIGHT NOW! DO YOU KNOW HOW EXCITED I WAS TO SUCK YOUR DICK TONIGHT? NO YOU DON'T BECAUSE YOU HAVE TO FUCKING WO...

I deleted that.

$imone: I won't lie Andre, I'm a little pissed off you know. How could you cancel last minute like that? Right now I'm wearing a Victoria's Secr...

I deleted that too.

$imone: So you mean no dick for me tonight? You're not gonna eat my pussy and watc...

Delete... I just needed to relax, relate and release. Shout out to Whitley Gilbert.

I tried one last time. Simple and emotionless.

$imone: Okay, no problem.

A whiff of Black Love incense wafted across my nose and I wanted to throw my fucking phone across the room.

'Okay...'

The room needed to change and now!

Closing my eyes, I inhaled the room and the moments I was planning when Andre got here. The way I wanted to moan in his face while I came on my dick... I mean his dick.

Awkward moment of silence here for calling his dick mine.

Shaking that off, I became a whirlwind in the living room, blowing out candles, turning the music off, putting the wine back in the fridge. Then taking it out again.

'Yeah we're gonna need THAT tonight for fuck's sake!'

I could feel the dressing gown flowing behind me and as sexy as I should've felt at that moment, or hoped Andre would make me feel, I was not feeling it.

Next stop, the bedroom to get out of this and into my tracksuit bottoms.

'For fuck's SAKE!'

I'd lost count of how many times I'd said for fuck's sake but it was at least five in the last five minutes.

I tossed the outfit and dressing gown on the floor then

imagined it crumpled there accompanied with my screams and stains on my bedsheets.

Then I saw it. On the comfy chair by my bed.

Andre's vest. The one he left here yesterday after our absolutely delectable episode in the bathroom. It was exactly like the *Soul Food* scene as well.

'FOR FUCK'S SAKE! Okay, that's the last one.'

Back in my tracksuit bottoms, holding the large grey Lonsdale vest, I held it to my face and inhaled deeply.

Suddenly, I was aroused as if he was there in the room with me. I stood there for a moment and shook my head.

'Oh for fuck's sake! Well we already know I'm gonna do this.'

Pulling my tracksuit bottoms to the floor, I sat back on my bed, pulled up pictures of Andre's dick from my gallery, opened the bottle of wine and spread my legs. Had to stop for a minute because my tracksuit bottoms were tangling my feet. I kicked them off frustratingly and got into a forced sexy groove.

This was NOT how I saw this night ending.

Andre's vest muzzled across my face, my fingers sliding through the wetness that built anticipating his arrival and my thumb scrolling through his dick pics.

This was not gonna be a good orgasm.

'For FUCK'S SAKE!'

Wednesday 7th February 2018

I am still saying for fuck's sake!

Work is NOT the place I want to be right now!

Channel 4 are MORE than involved with the documentary

and have accepted the changes we've made. We've wrapped on all scenes and interviews, re-enactments and research and are close to finishing post-production. So it's a mad house around the office right now and all the mad people seem to be running their madness by me. And as I just said, work is NOT the place I want to be right now!

Functioning I was but focussed I wasn't. Everyone around me was feeling I wasn't in a good mood and gave me a wide berth. My mind was playing all kinds of tricks on me and every Andre moment was playing in a remix of moments. Every kiss, lick, bite, spank, strangle played in a mix-up of scenes that would not leave me the fuck alone. And I needed them too.

You know why? Because for some reason, I couldn't get Andre on the phone. No morning text, no follow-up convo about how his day started, no gif battles for us to engage in.

All I got from him this morning was...

Andr3: GM

That's it!

That's all the fuck I got from him this morning. Since then, Nathan.

I've responded with a proper good morning and update on the day ahead, with sly shots about my disappointment about the night before and he hasn't said shit back. He hasn't even read the message yet. And I've been checking all morning and nothing. I haven't even caught him online, which means he's not talking to anyone on his phone. Does that mean he's not NEAR his phone or maybe he's using it for something else? Maybe he 's using it to record a sloppy blowjob that he's getting from some random BITCH he's fucking instead of me?

I gave that last one some major thought. There could be no way in London heaven that a man with a dick that blessed and a sex game so boom ting isn't fucking someone else out there. He's like gold dust. AND he can hold a conversation. AND he listens. AND he's eats me out with effort and verve. Some woman out there was probably getting what I was due and was probably cumming and laughing at the same time. Or his work thing could be real and I could be just really tired after a terrible night's rest.

I swear, I woke out my sleep randomly and shouted out, 'FOR FUCK'S SAKE!'

My laptop in front of me had sixteen Google Chrome tabs open and the main one was a Google Search page and I typed in Andre's name.

'WHAT THE FUCK!?'

I looked around at no-one in particular and screwed up my eyebrows in a nasty way then shook my head.

'I don't know his surname!'

How this just dawned on me I'll never know but then that could've been why I couldn't find him on social media.

Like, how the fuck did I just clock that I don't know his surname?

The man had been inside me. Skin to skin, multiple times and I didn't even know his surname?

'HOW do I not know the dude's surname for fuck's sake?'

I couldn't understand how I let this happen. Hadn't I ever asked him his surname? Did I ask and he deflect the question onto something else?

My first instinct was to go back to the source, which was

my sister who hooked us up in the first place. But I didn't want her to know that I didn't know something as simple as his fucking surname.

His FUCKING surname for fuck's sake.

Staring at the screen with his name in the search box and nothing else.

Checking our message box, he still hadn't read my message. One tick.

What the fuck was he doing?

I needed, I mean wanted to hear from him, just to know that he was okay. It'd only been like, what, 15 hours, nine minutes and 16 seconds ago since his last message. A little courtesy doesn't cost a thing.

Closing the tab, I locked my phone, put on a random Spotify playlist and threw myself into my work. The hope was that the work would distract me.

It didn't.

The rest of my day was shit... nothing got better, my workload took me out of the office and every handsome black man I walked past looked like Andre. I banged through my work with the desire of a woman possessed. Not by dick unfortunately. My manager gave me the rest of the afternoon off and I chose to spend it in the gym.

There was a LOT of frustration to work off.

Andre was YET to read my message from the morning AND my afternoon follow-up.

Nothing. Not even online for fuck's sake.

Where the fuck was he? Because he wasn't doing me and that was proving to be a problem. My arms after extra sets of chin-ups were also a problem for me and I took a moment bent over trying to catch my breath.

Every time my phone vibrated in my arm-clasp, I was on it like a flash. I went straight to Andre's chat but nothing. I found a empty running machine, rose the inclination and said fuck the warm-up and went straight for a speedy jog.

My phone vibrated again and I checked the message on my watch while frustrated sweat began to run down my temple. I unhooked my phone and, as usual, went straight to Andre. He'd written a message and deleted it.

'WHAT THE FUCK?'

Jumping off the treadmill without missing a beat, I pulled my earphones out and scrutinised my phone like it owed me six month's rent.

According to What's App, he was online but that was it. He'd read my messages from the morning and the afternoon, said something but he decided to DELETE IT? What the fuck did it say?

Huffing and puffing, lording over my phone, I inhaled deeply as it said Andre was writing something.

I smiled stupidly at my phone and waited.

And waited.

The treadmill was still running and I slammed the emergency stop button.

Still waiting.

My smile was shaking into a frown.

STILL waiting. He was still writing.

'SAY SOMETHING FOR FUCK'S SAKE!' I shouted at my phone. I took a second to look around to make sure no-one was looking at me like I was crazy.

Back to my phone and he was STILL writing. Like what

the fuck did he have to say that had him writing so fucking much?

And he was still writing!

I'd never suffered an anxiety attack or had problems with being calm but this was killing me. I was tense all over, my mind was decided and undecided at the same time, I wasn't focussed on my workout any more and I was angry at my phone.

Andr3: Hey Simone. I'm so sorry I've been M.I.A. all day. That work emergency has gone on longer than it should. I've been dealing with firewalls and corresponding servers all day and I'm tired. How are you?

My hand gripped my phone so tightly.

All that typing and that's all he had to say?

Firewalls and servers? So he worked with computers then? Okay great but where the fuck was the rest of the message? Did he write something and then delete it? There had to be more than this. How am I? Where's my dick?!

My thumbs got ready to reply and he said something else.

Andr3: I really miss you right now. It's a shame I didn't get to come down and do you something sexy.

So then fucking tell me when you can come round and do what you do! What, was I the only one who thought that? If he wanted me and he missed me, he would make a plan to come and get some right?

Don't just miss me, fuck me!

I grabbed the bull by the horns.

$imone: So why don't you stop missing me and come and fuck me?

He read the message and his 'online' status disappeared.

'OH DON'T YOU FUCKING...'

My fingers moved so quickly across the keyboard in anger and frustration, I wrote a long nothing of a word that had numbers in it.

I deleted it.

$imone: If you're free tonight, so am I... anytime.

Hoping the message would bring him back online, I felt out of place in the gym since I had no inspiration to work out any more.

From the gym to my place, I stared at my phone, rereading his last messages, analysing the times he sent them, calculating how much time in between messages, checking his words for spelling mistakes and groaning every time I'd scroll up to a dick pic.

I stayed sat in my corner spot on the sofa until 11pm staring at Andre's profile picture, which was a picture of Roll Safe's classic meme 'thinking' picture. There was not one aspect of our conversations I didn't replay in my head. I scrolled to the very first message he sent me and I read up to today's absolute tease of a message. And yet, here I am, still staring at my phone just hoping he'd read my messages and reply. If he'd read it, he'd know there was no problem with his coming over.

And still FUCKING NOTHING FROM HIM!

'AND STILL FUCKING NOTHING!'

Thursday 8th February 2018

The way my sleep is set up, I have like eight alarms set with about 15-20 minutes in between each one. On this particular morning, I woke up before every alarm and what do you think my first port of call was?

That's right, Andre's messages. And guess what? Nothing since our extremely brief, less than arousing exchange yesterday. Well, it wasn't less than arousing because seeing him type something made me imagine the words said in his sexy tone. And his voice is fucking sexy!

He hadn't even read the "come over anytime" message which is why I've woken up on my bed with his vest strewn across my legs.

I attached my phone to its charger and sighed with heavy exasperation on my pillow looking up at the ceiling. It was too early to be awake but not late enough to go back to sleep. Five more minutes of sleep could accidentally become 45 minutes and I'd be late. Again.

I'm not usually like that. I'm always first one in, last one out but Andre's distracting dick has got me sleeping later and waking up even later. And, like last night, I'm now having frustrating masturbation moments with myself. Looking down at my legs, I could feel the dried stains of the moment I squirted while rubbing Andre's vest on my clit but... it just wasn't the same. Sure I could smell him and I was flicking between pictures of him and voice notes he'd sent me, but the moment I came… it just wasn't… it didn't hit that spot I needed it to.

I don't remember much about the night after that.

Feeling drained, not sure whether physically or emotionally, I rolled off my bed, past my tracksuit bottoms on the floor and shuffled to the bathroom. Maybe starting my day early would put some groove in my soul and I could at least feel like I was functioning like a normal human being.

Because right now I didn't feel like myself.

Turning the hot water tap past the point where I usually like it, I watched steaming hot water flow into the bath and a really powerful flashback hit me. It was so visual, so physical, so real, I had to sit down on the toilet to enjoy it.

The memory was from the day Andre came round while I was on the phone to work. At some point during that night we ended up in the shower together and the dude washed me from head to toe. He causes absolute bliss with his hands so I was his at that point. Then he rinsed me. You wanna know how free he made me feel at that moment?

I let him wash my hair!

I wasn't planning to get my hair wet either. My hair is natural and only comes down to my ears but the way I do this and that and twist this and fold that, you would think I had dreadlocks, such is my talent with my hair. But, as I said, I wasn't planning to wash my hair that night. When we got in the shower, I put my shower cap on and between him scrubbing me up and rinsing me down, it came off and I was lounging in his arms as he supported my lower back and ass cheeks and hot water peppered my scalp with stinging rain. The flashback was live in my mind as I looked at the bar on the side where I put my foot to allow him to slip into me.

Bending over with his hands running up and down my back and his dick swirling inside me... yes swirling. Andre has good dick control so he likes to slide just about halfway inside me then spin his hips so the dick sort of comes in from the left and slides out from the right then back in a circle again. You ever have a guy do that to you ladies? It is the SHIT!

Fellas, you ever done that to a woman? If you have then you're a brown-eyed demon like Andre is. Well he's not a demon, he's a chocolate wonder probably created in the deepest pits of Wakanda and sent to destroy my life.

A random shiver/body ripple ran through me all of a sudden and I mumbled as if the Spirit took me.

'Shumunakuvasiminaboobooo...'

Right, job one. Get that memory the fuck out of my mind, job two, get dressed and get active.

I looked my naked self in the mirror and sighed at the Sainsburys bags growing under my eyes.

'You look like shit!'

'Yeah well, it's not my fault. If he'd just come round and given me a dose of that gooooooood...'

I trailed off into a groan, ran the water in the sink and, I'll tell you, I've never brushed my teeth with such anger in all my life. I caught myself looking mad and it tickled me a bit but I didn't laugh.

Job one wasn't completed and I spent the whole shower thinking about what I was trying to forget. I even closed my eyes for crying out loud.

'FOR FUCK'S SAKE!' I yelled as shower water dripped into my mouth.

If there's anyone keeping count on just how many times

I've screamed shouted or said 'for fuck's sake' because of this guy, please let me know.

My usual five-minute shower was cut down to a speedy three minutes. Andre's fault. The memories were pissing me off.

I wiped myself down, fighting to ignore the moment he dried my 34D breasts and I came. I didn't tell him and it honestly snuck out from nowhere.

Instinct told me to check my phone.

'Oi oiiiiiiiiii…' I sang with gun fingers as my towel dropped to the floor.

Andre read my message. The two blue ticks next to my message told me so.

'Come on then… cheer up my morning you prick!'

I rushed to the bedroom, laid my phone on my bed carefully and reached for knickers, socks, a t-shirt and jeans from my wardrobe and shot back to my phone. Bent at the hips, the way Andre liked me, I was staring at those two blue ticks like they were Andre's dick appearing through the phone. My eyes were wide, waiting for my phone to tell me he was online. What would he say to me? How would he say good morning? He always said something different when it came to his morning greetings but they were always filled with a new nickname that related to something we'd done the night before. Lethal Lipps 2.5, Foetal Nite Nite, Disney Eyes, Skills-A-Lot and Miss Bendy Nuh Rass were some of the names he called me, which always made me belly laugh in the morning.

It was strange how much energy I suddenly felt and I played Sza and Dram's *Caretaker*. My hips were swaying as I sang along, rubbing coconut oil into my hands and over my skin, still staring at my phone hoping something would happen while I was looking at it.

Dressing in record time - *I Am Wakanda* t-shirt, fitted jeans, wrapped hair, and Jordan Flight 45's in black and pink - I two-stepped to the kitchen while singing along to King's *Hey*. When the beat kicked in, I was spinning around, grabbing milk, a bowl and a box of Crunchy Nut. Due to my grinding motions, I was spilling milk on the side but I didn't care, stealing quick looks at my phone.

'Cooooooooome onnnnn,' I yelled at my phone, bringing it up to my face.

I scrolled across to the girls group and hoped some of my ladies would be up. Of course I wouldn't tell them I was fiending for this guy like...

My lips stuck out duck style and I stopped what I was doing and looked up to think. Russia's 'dickmatised' speech came back to my head and I was lost in thought. I mean, it's only the 7th right and we've only... no it's the 8th and we've only been fucking since the 2nd of February... sliding into the 3rd right? So how in any way, shape or form can I be addicted to this guy in five days? Are you crazy? What am I sixteen? Fuck off. I am a grown ass, paying my own bills and doing my thing black woman with firm thighs and a wicked credit score. There is no way on God's green earth, I could be addicted to a man's penis in only five days. And he's not my man. No, no, sorry, I don't buy it. I obviously don't know how truly weak Russia and Katrina have been for dick in the past but I know that's not me. I mean yeah I miss it but I'm not like PINING for it... it would just take the edge off, you know? Like a straight double Wray and Nephews after a long day.

I stood against the counter with my bowl of cereal, keeping an eye on the spilled milk I'd ignored on the counter. I squinted at it, put my bowl down and got a strip of kitchen roll and wiped it up with a quick vigour that took me by surprise.

'Dickmatised you know? Is that even a real word?'

There was an urge to ask the girls but they were now awake and talking about *Black Panther* which we were all going to see tomorrow. Some creative genius on social media came up with the idea that black people should attend the screening wearing something representing African culture. Tomorrow was the premier at Stratford Vue and we'd booked our tickets the morning they went on sale. I got this dress made… oooo you should see it. Handmade in Nigeria thanks to an extra few days following an interview for the Tatiana Blue documentary. It hugs me like Andre did when he was fucking me in the bathroom when the girls were here and he was about to cum and he pulled out and slid his dick between my cheeks and came on my back while the girls in the living room were shouting out 'eyyy eyyyyyy eyyyyyyyyy'. That was a sweet moment.

'That guy,' I said to myself shaking my head.

I checked my phone and he was online. I was about to take my last spoonful of cereal when my hand stopped right before it got to my mouth. My eyes widened, stomach growled - totally unrelated - and I felt like I was literally hanging on the edge of a cliff. Like that moment in *Eastenders* at Christmas when Lauren started to fall off the roof and you thought 'oh ohhh there she goes… and she's taking the other one with her too'. That was sooooo funny. Me and my girls were making hella noise at Christmas over that one.

Putting my bowl in the sink, I watched as Andre had not only come online but he was typing something and I did a little steppity-step and jazz hands. My hands spread across the counter and I dipped my face close to my phone, calculating the time it would take me to type something. I'm not the speediest with my fingers on a keyboard but I can get a good thick paragraph out in under three minutes. So I know how much I'm expecting to read when he is says typing for like 30 seconds. In 30 seconds, I can give you a pretty detailed breakdown of my day from morning to night and throw something dirty in between. So far, Andre had been "typing" for 47 seconds. I would forgo all the good morning niceties and just read about a time when I could have him inside me. THAT was necessary. THAT was needed. And now.

'Yeah that boy knows what the fuck he's doing,' I said to myself and rolled my neck like a kitten being scratched.

And yes, I am fully aware that for the second day in a row, I am staring at my phone WAITING for this guy to say something. That doesn't mean anything, I just miss... the closeness. I mean dedicated, undivided, night and day attention and then, for two days, nothing? Of course I'm gonna miss it.

The sun was rising on what looked like a cold day so I reminded myself to pick up my scarf and giant winter hat, which fit nicely over my headwraps.

Sneering at my phone, I put it in my pocket and got my work things together. Post production had wrapped and we were, apparently, going to be able to see the first cut of the documentary. This was a big thing for me because the idea for the documentary was originally my idea and I've managed to bring it through pitching, production, even getting Channel 4 involved so this is huge for my career at this time. And this was the plan. Stay at the production company long enough to learn the ropes, grow in the position then take over or start my own. I felt there were a lot of stories not being told due to the colour of the main character and I wanted to change that.

Yeah, fully Issa Rae inspired. Oh shit, that reminds me, I've got the last two episodes of *Insecure* to watch. And Kojo's *The Weekend.*

In a long grey chequered winter coat, scarf, hat and gloves and work bag, I was ready to go. By the time I got in, I'd be a full hour and a half early but I was starting to feel like I needed to get out of the house. Everywhere I looked had an Andre memory connected to it. Especially my corner spot. Oh shit, he's ruined that place for me now. It was Skype day. He made me tap out and have to hold a pillow over my face to muffle how fucking loud I was being.

Shaking the memory away, I picked up my keys and walked out of the door, locking it behind me.

I checked my phone again and Andre was STILL typing.

'Flipping hell... this better be a blow-by-blow account of how much you've missed me and what you're gonna do to me TONIGHT ANDRE... TONIGHT!'

My voice echoed in the corridor and I put my head down and started walking to the lifts.

'No, but for real, what the FUCK are you typing that you've been typing for this long though? This is ridiculous.'

The middle of three carriages opened and I got in, pressing the ground floor multiple times, feeling annoyance growing.

Checking again, he was STILL typing.

Like come on.

Unless... What if he isn't typing his deepest, sexiest thoughts about me? What if he's typing out the long way of telling me that he doesn't want to fuck me any more. I bet he's found a girlfriend... or maybe he's fucking someone else and she's better than me. Well, I DON'T think that's possible because I'm not bad.

Fucking Andre and his making me feel sexy and confident and shit.

I'd never tell him that though... that's just between us. But yeah, he has. I don't know how but he has.

The lift opened to the ground floor and the lobby of the reception area was full of people dressed in black with mournful faces. My instant instincts told me there was a funeral and this was the meeting point.

Bit early for a funeral but okay.

I excused myself through the crowd of races all dressed in black and made it to the door while taking a look at my phone.

Andr3: Good morning you...

'ARE YOU ABSOLUTELY FUCKING KIDDDING?!' I shouted while holding the door open.

I closed my eyes and sighed heavily. I didn't need to turn around to know that everyone was looking at me. The dead silence that followed my outburst told me all I needed to know.

But, for real, all that typing and all he had to say for

himself was *'good morning you*? Was he taking the piss out of my life? Like, honestly? From the kitchen, I was able to get my stuff for work, put my cold shit on, come DOWNSTAIRS and he was typing all that time and all he said was *'good morning you'?*

I'm feeling like a side plate of onion rings at the moment.

Dipping my head in respect, I raised my hand to the people who were still looking at me.

'Sorry, about that. Have a nice day.'

They're going to a funeral, why the fuck would I say have a nice day?

God, my head is all over the place!

Friday 9th February 2018

'BUT THE SHOES DON'T MATCH... JUST LIKE YOUR LAST THREE BOYFRIENDS!'

Fire was spilling out of my mouth into my bedroom while me and my girls got ready together over the phone. I looked myself up and down in my one-of-a-kind, made only for me dress. Boob-tube top half and fitted, to the knee lower half with a split that I, at first, thought was too high, but now I like it. The material... it looks like blue flames.

It is *Black Panther* night and, don't mind me saying so, I look good.

Good enough to eat... well I would be good enough to eat if someone came and...

Nope... not tonight. Tonight, I belonged to Prince T'Challa... no KING T'Challa and he was going to take me on a mystical magic ride of black excellence, directed by black excellence and fully representing? You guessed it, black excellence.

My afro-pick earrings went with the outfit perfectly as did my Charlotte Oympia shoes, which deserved an outing after the last time I put them on and NO-ONE saw them.

Andre, as seems to be the norm now, has been quiet. A bit more chatty but not like he was when this thing of ours kicked off. Today was day three of 'No-Andre-Penis-Making-Me-Feel-Good' or NAPMMFG. Three days, seven hours and nine minutes if anyone is keeping count.

'How we looking ladies?' Russia said humming to herself.

'I'm already out the door,' Katrina said. 'Last queen there has to sleep with Ulysees Klaue.'

'Nah sah... ah di king mi cum fah...' I shouted while picking up my phone and my handbag. 'I bet Brina is gonna be the last one there.'

On cue, my sister's voice appeared in the conversation. 'Yeah, I'll just meet you guys there. Why the fuck does this dickhead have to start arguing with me now? He knows how important this night is and he waits until now to want to talk about our "relationship"? Fuck off! Doesn't he know the fate of Wakanda hangs in the balance?'

'Sis, you've got no chill. Give him some head and leave just as he's about to cum. He won't know what hit him.'

'Damn Sim! And you say I've got no chill.'

'Look what the dick has made of her ladies!' Russia said prophetically.

'Up yours and your foolish dickmatised theory. For the record, it's been three days since I got some and I'm doing fine. No cocaine-like withdrawals, no fiending, I've just been getting on with things.'

'Thou dost protest too much!'

'FUCK YOU RUSSIA... See you lot there.'

I hung up the phone on our group call and looked at myself in the mirror one last time while stuffing my keys into my clutch purse, which was also made of the same material.

TO MAAAAAAAAAAAAAATCCCH...

I could spot one strand of hair unrolling from the nine chiney-bumps around my head... with only the neatest of partings by the way.

Yes yes yes, I felt good. And I looked good.

I didn't feel like I was lying when I told the girls that I was doing good without Andre's dick. I think I've been doing okay.

I twirled in the mirror and chanted with a chuckle.

'WAKANDA FOREVER!'

Excited wasn't the word for what was running through me at that moment. If we're sharing things, I'm an old school secret comic book nerd. Since the early 80s... I used to read all of them, especially Black Panther. Because he was one of only a few black superheroes in a mainly white superhero world. And not only that, he had his own country and they came with their own stories as well. And now it's being turned into a movie with an all-black cast as well? Fuck off... I'm there.

And, I look damn fucking good too. I really do!

'I should send him a picture of how good I look... no, fuck him, if he can't find out how I'm doing or be arranging a dicking then fuck him.'

I said it but I also wanted him to fuck... me.

The urge, the hunger, the damn near almost crippling desire to even just kiss him was there in the pit of my stomach but I held it there. Chadwick Bosman, Michael B. 'eat me please' Jordan, Lupita, Danai, Forest the legend, Angela the queen of everything, even my man from *Get Out.* I can never remember his name but I love him same way. Those were the people that were bubbling my excitement and making me almost skip to my front door. Looking at my watch, then checking my cab app, I could tell I was going to be early but that would've been okay. Least I wouldn't be fucking Ulysees Claue.

Opening the door, remembering the scenes from the trailers that I was most looking forward to, an instant presence stopped me in my tracks.

'Miss Simone looking... wow.'

His voice registered in the back of my THROAT for fuck sake before I even saw him. Yes, the back of my throat. His voice travelled all through my shit, from my toes to my nipples and all in between and into the back of my throat.

God... for fuck's sake... what is it about this guy's voice that just.... grrrrrrr.

By the time I looked at him, he was staring me up and down. Not a quick look either, he was LOOKING ME UPPPPPPPP AND DOOOOOOOOOOWN. Oh he was enjoying himself, lemme tell you. I could see it all over him. He covered his mouth and was leaning to look around me... My ass DID look good in this dress.

The man looked frozen.

'Andre... well hello stranger. Finally woke up from your deep sleep huh?'

Instinct made me attack, my thighs wanted to open for him right then and there though. I was ready to fight and fuck at the same time.

'I deserved that. Look, I'm sorry I haven't been...'

'Hold on, how did you get in the building?'

'Oh someone coming out and let me in.'

'They're not allowed to do that. We've had so many meetings about letting random people into the building. So many useless, long ass...'

And then he kissed me. Fucking Andre kissed me.

Three days, seven hours and 16 minutes later but that's neither here nor there.

He didn't smush his face into mine in order to shut me up with the kiss... he searched. The kiss was a grace... a brush of his lips against mine. When my lips parted, he'd brush his bottom lip between them and kiss me. That is... some NEXT type of kiss and whatever anger and frustration I had built up fell as my lips responded to his and I slid a hand around his neck. This all happened so quickly, I hadn't even closed my front door.

'Where you going looking so yummy?'

I didn't answer him... I held his face in my hand and looked into his eyes... what for, I don't know but I did. His eyes contained sorrow and something he wasn't saying. He broke my hold and kissed me heavily this time, making us quick step back into my apartment. I slammed the door shut over his shoulder as we held the kiss and swerved our way through my living room. Then we stopped.

'Andre, where have you been for the last three days? What's going on?'

'It's a long story. It all started with work that day. What happened was...'

For some reason he couldn't talk while I was unbuckling his jeans.

He looked down and watched my hands, expert now at unbuckling his belt and popping his buttons.

'Yeah,' I mumbled. 'So carry on. It all started with work that day. What happened at work that day?'

'Our entire system shut down and...'

Again, he couldn't seem to focus as I opened his buttons by pulling my hands apart. I liked that 'prrrrrrr' sound. His eyes were locked on mine as I dipped very very slowly, making sure he was watching me on the way down. We both pulled his trousers and boxers to his ankles.

'Yeaaaaaah, whole system shut down AND?'

'And I had to basically not just reset our entire system, I had to reBUILD...'

'You're gonna have to learn to focus Andre.'

His dick flopped over my wrist and, after a few subtle squeezes, he was hard in my grip.

'Listen, I didn't come here just to fuck you, I wanted to at least give you the courtesy of coming to see you and apologising...'

My mouth took him all the way in and he wide-eyed stared at me.

His arms rose like he was showing off his muscles and that's when I knew I had his attention. My bag slid off my arm and I lowered it to the floor as I got onto my knees. There was something sexy about what was going on right now. Me in my sexiest of dresses and heels on my knees with a dick in my mouth. An idea caught up to me and I opened my eyes.

I popped the dick out of my mouth and jumped to my feet, pushing Andre backwards from the waist. He went with me until my floor-to-ceiling windows stopped him. He looked back at the London skyline and I looked around his hips, admiring the red and white lights across the night-time landscape.

'Good thing you've got...'

I didn't let him finish his sentence and took him back into my mouth, this time squatting in front of him. Holding his growing dick with my lips, I parted my legs and pulled my dress back over my thighs so he could see... or not see. Andre was a fan of a tease so he appreciated my thighs being open while sucking his dick so he could imagine my pussy just there... waiting to be looked at or played with.

With London looking sexy behind us, I pictured where I should've been at that point in my originally planned evening. According to the time, I was gonna be fucking Ulysees Claue, which might not be a bad thing if he can change the thing on his arm to a dildo with three-speed settings.

Andre's hips were moving back and forth, feeding me his dick.

I stopped again. Stood up and went to my bathroom where I took a black hand towel and draped it over my shoulder. I came back to Andre leaning against the window and stepping out of his trousers with his three legs looking all muscular.

'Weren't you going somewhere?'

I made sure the rest of my walk towards him was nothing but Angela Bassett sexy as I took the black hand towel and tied it around my neck and squatted in front of him again.

With a quick deep breath, I took his whole eight... maybe nine inches with a curve and didn't stop until my lips touched his stomach. With my eyes innocently looking up at his.

He knew good and damn well I wasn't going anywhere

tonight.

My girls were gonna kill me!

T'Challa forgive me!

Saturday 10th February 2018

For the second time in the row, I woke up before my alarms. Reaching over to turn them off, I found Andre's heaving chest blocking me. Heaving up and down after a massive, epic, spiritual moment last night.

Ladies, we didn't fuck last night, we made LOVE!

Yes there is a difference. Hold on, lemme charge my phone and I'll break it down.

Wait, hold on, where is my phone?

I traced my steps over the last night and, in the dark, scooted out of my sheets and felt on the floor. My memory told me that the last time I remember even registering my phone was after we made six videos, recording some shit that I can't WAIT to watch again.

Under strewn clothes, I felt my phone and brought it to life.

'12%? Fucccck...'

The urge to pee took me over before I knew it and I was creeping out of my room and into the bathroom where I sat down with a silent siiiiiigh.

A shiver ran down my spine and a yawn crept over me. I stretched my arms over my head and groaned in pain, remembering the moments Andre held me down with a serious kung-fu grip and offered the slowest of strokes I've ever had from a dick. You wanna know how slow it was? If you've ever been to a dance... I'm talking about a rare grooves kinda dance. And you find that someone to get that wall-scrubbing dance with? And you've both got your foreheads against each other and you're both just watching the slow whine. You know when it gets REAL SLOW like you're barely even moving? The strokes were that slow.

He. Slayed. My. Pussy!

There was no doubt about it. Chadwick Bosman and the man dem were going to have to understand because I came in ways that I'm even embarrassed to tell you about.

Wipe, flush, wash hands, dressing gown off the back of the door and I was in need of a hot drink.

Tying the drawstring around my waist and stretching out my legs, I snuck playfully out of the bathroom, high on the memories and the physical niggles I felt as a result of the man sleeping in my bed. And he deserved a good moment of sleep. To be honest, I felt like I wasn't meant to be on my feet and would take my hot drink back to bed with me. Maybe make him a cup of tea to wake up to.

Knowing my way around my furniture, I walked into the living room without turning on a light, passing my centre table on the way to the kitchen. I turned the kitchen light on, emptied and refilled the kettle - which was hot for some reason - and got it boiling. One cup of coffee for me and cup of tea, probably two sugars, for Andre.

'You making him breakfast too?'

The voice from out of fucking nowhere made me jump. Don't ask me why I looked straight up as if the voice was coming from the heavens but I did.

I recognised it as Brina's voice and checked my phone to make sure I hadn't called her by accident then walked to the living room and turned the light on.

Brina was sitting in the dark with a cup of something in her hands.

'Why the fuck are you sitting in the dark like some serial killer?'

'So you ARE alive then?'

'Huh, what'd you mean?'

My crap response made me turn back to the two hot drinks I now had to sneak past my sister and into the bedroom. Although sneaking was out.

Shit, what if Andre wakes up and walks in naked thinking its only us here?

'Where were you supposed to be last night? Where did you SAY you were on your way to last night before you fell off the face of the fucking earth? Which three of the most sexiest Wakanda-representing queens were you supposed to race to the cinema last night?'

'Yeah I know, I know... I just suddenly came over all sick and...'

'SIMONE DENISE McKENZIE... are you about to start lying to me?'

She stood up and walked into the kitchen, staring at my back. I could feel her staring at me.

'No sis... I just...'

'OH... no no no... let's go down the road you were gonna travel. Okay, so you were sick huh?'

'No, I...'

The kettle was boiling.

'Yeah, you were sick... you weren't feeling well. What did you take for you ailment? How many times did you TAKE it sis? Huh? Did you take any vitamins for this ailment, this sickness that attacked you all of a sudden? Huh?! Did you take any vitamins? Any vitamin A? No, B? No, C? No... oh well if you didn't take any of those then you MUST'VE taken some vitamin D, right Sim?'

The counter was rumbling and steam rose as I tied my hair in a long loose plait. I turned around to say something but the look on Brina's face made me burst out into a random, raucous laugh.

'It was vitamin S actually,' I whispered and tried to tone it down to a giggle.

'Sim you missed *Black Panther*?! Not some any random Marvel film... *Black Panther* for fuck's sake!? You should've seen it... black people came out looking beautiful. So many colourful outfits, headties - which had to come off during the film - oh it was amazing. You should've seen it, the film was so damn good. Oh wait, you were supposed to but you didn't turn up. You didn't even call anyone to say "I'm okay, I just tripped but I'm using some dick to feel better..." - nothing.'

'It's not a crutch...'

'Sis, you are ATTACHED to this dick!'

The kettle boiled and Brina grabbed me by the shoulders.

'I am not...'

'You ARE dickmatised little sister. You are. Look at you, you look tired, bags under your eyes, late for shit, cancelling without prior warning OR follow-up call to let us know you're okay? You're place isn't looking as spotless as it usually is, he's now staying round and...'

She paused and I slid out of her arms to pour the drinks. I knew where her mind would take her and I had to think of an answer before she asked.

'Are you using protection with all this rampant fucking

you're doing at the moment?'

'Don't be stupid. Of course I am...'

'Simone!?'

'We ARE... I swear.'

She spun me around, making me spill the second sugar I was putting in his tea.

'What are you doing uhhhhh?'

'Look me in the eyes and tell me you are using protection?!'

If I looked her in the eyes, she would've known right away. If I tried to look away, that would've been an instant admittance of guilt.

Shiiiiiiit...

'I know how many condoms you got in your drawer you know.'

'How do you know THAT?'

'I'm your sister!'

'Erm, so?!'

I went with option A and tried to shoot a steely-eyed shot.

Steadying my tired eyes, I met her stare.

'I AM using protection Brina, I promise.'

I watched her eyes dart from my left to my right eye, searching from the truth. Being the younger sister, I learned everything about lies from her so she always knew if I was lying.

Every time.

'Hmmm... I don't know if you're telling the truth or your dickmatised state is making you a better liar.'

'I am NOT dickmatised for fuck's sake!'

She finished her drink and put her cup in the sink.

'See look, plates and shit in the sink? That's not you.' She scoffed 'You know what one of the worst things is about being dickmatised? The denial. The thinking that you have everything in control.'

'I do.'

'Do you?'

Her demeanour changed and she folded her arms and snaked her neck.

I worried when she did that.

'Yeaaah, I can stand here in my dressing gown and proudly say that I am not addicted to Andre's dick.' I ended my sentence with a definitive head nod to book-end my truth.

My wavering truth.

'So you mean to tell me that if I went in that room right now and fucked Andre, you wouldn't feel any sort of way?'

Just hearing the question made the emotional equivalent of my life crumple inside me. Oh shit, it was like atomic bomb damage to everything inside me. Fuck who and live where? She wouldn't dare...

But what I also had to do was act like I didn't give a shit.

Andre wasn't my boyfriend nor did I envision him getting that spot. ALTHOUGH, in saying that, I did think about what life would be like with Andre as my man. It was quite blissful thinking actually.

'Well, first of all sis, that would be breaking queen rules in fucking another queen's fuck buddy or friend's with benefits.'

'Yeah, but I'm asking permission so it's not the same right?'

Brina picked up my cup of coffee and sipped it, watching every move of my face. Her lips were on the cusp of smiling as she watched me squirm. And she knew. I knew she knew.

And she knew that I knew she knew.

Andre was mine and I didn't want ANYONE else fucking him, let alone my married sister. 'I wouldn't care because Andre is just helping me scratch an itch.'

'SO, if I went in there and scratched an itch of my own, you'd be okay with that?'

'Sis, I'd IMPLORE you too. It's quite good.'

'Yeah, it's having an AMAZING effect on you so far.'

WHY THE FUCK DID I SAY THAT?

My ego was saying things my heart wasn't. There was no way I would be okay with my sister fucking Andre. But she'd put me in a position where I had nothing to say. If I said I wasn't okay with it, then it would subscribe to her theory that I was dickmatised. If I said I was okay with it then I had to deal with the fact that my sister may just actually go and fuck Andre?

Brina was 'fuck-it-all' like that sometimes. And with her husband Donovan misbehaving on a regular basis, she could be at the point of saying fuck it.

She was killing me with the eyes. Scanning my face and my body language for any awkwardness that I was trying to hold inside.

Frowning, I safely snatched my drink back from her and held it to my chest.

'So, what, can I go and borrow your friend for a minute?'

She clapped her hands and stepped side-to-side like she was preparing for a race. This was turning from something that felt like a joke into something that seemed like it could actually happen.

I squinted briefly at her, seething at the position she put

me in.

I mean, I was not dickmatised... or addickted... or hooked on the D or whatever my girls liked to call it. I was just happy with what I had and wanted to continue doing it. Does that mean I'm addicted? I mean the craziest thought I'd had about his dick was cutting it off and keeping it but that was it. Nothing crazier than that.

'Just make sure you take my sheets off the bed when you're done.'

Brina recoiled with wide eyes and leaned back. 'Whoaaa, you REALLY are hooked on this thing aren't you? You are lying through your front, back and side teeth. Aaaawww sis, you don't even know it either, that's the worst thing.'

'For the last time,' I started. 'I am NOT fucking addicted! Go head, see for yourself. For all the shit Donovon has put you through, this is a Tic-Tac in the ocean. Go for it.'

She wasn't saying anything, just looking at me. Reading me like a fucking book. And she taught me to read as a child so... you know... funny.

'You don't think I won't go in there and fuck that guy sleeping in your bed? As horny as I've been?'

'You and Donovan on another sex break?'

'Has the last sex break ended though?'

I held my hands over my mouth.

'Shiiiiiiiit...'

'You know what sis? I think I'm gonna do it. Right now.'

Whoa, hold up... what the fuck did she just say to me?

'Do what sis?'

'To have sex with Andre. I could really do with a nice orgasm. You sure you don't mind?'

She turned to walk off to my bedroom and I reached out to stop her, while still trying to be cool. 'No, wait... you sure you wanna do this? Just because Donovan cheats, doesn't mean you have to do it too?'

'Oh no I WANT to do it. You won't say anything will you?'

WHAT THE FUCK WAS SHE DOING?

Not only did she want to fuck my man... my fuck buddy I mean... but she wanted me to keep it a secret from her husband as well. That last part wasn't hard because I didn't care for Donovan that much. But the first was killing me.

'No of course not, get yours sis. I'm gonna have a shower. Could you erm... I don't know... not get anything on my sheets please? This is already weird enough.'

WHY WAS I SAYING THESE THINGS?

I didn't mean any of them.

That fucking corner she put me in.... grrrr.... it kills me.

She knew there was no way I would let her feel like she was right, even though she wasn't. And to prove that to her, I had to offer her a taste off my plate. Excessive?

'Okay, I'm going then... I'm gooooooing to fuck Andre!'

'Condoms are in the top draw next to the bed.'

'Yeah I know.'

'No problem. Get yours sis.'

OH JUST SHUT THE FUCK UP ALREADY... is what I was screaming inside my head. How had we gone from this would never happen to me telling her where I kept my condoms. My thoughts stopped when she took one last look at me, read the feelings all over my face and disappeared.

I listened. Listened to her walk away through the living room. Listened to her open the living room door. Listened to her light steps arrive at and OPEN my bedroom door.

It opened and closed.

'Did she actually just go off to fuck Andre? OH MY GOD…' I put a hand over my mouth. 'For fuuuuuuuck's sake… oh sis, tell me you didn't go in my room…'

I gathered myself, stood up straight and took careful steps through the living room with a quick few in the middle. I quietly opened the door and tried to use my best hearing to see if she had truly gone in my room.

Tip-toeing to the bathroom, I turned the taps on and ran the shower. Another few quick steps and I had my ear pressed to my own bedroom door like some peeping fucking Tom. Andre's growl was undeniable and I pulled my own hair, felt like I was about to implode and ran back to the bathroom for the hottest and longest shower of my motherfucking life.

I am NOT addicted!

Sunday 11th February 2018

What is a nervous-wreck? No honestly, like what is a nervous-wreck? What does one look like? How do they operate? What gets them through the day?

I'm not saying I am one… oh don't worry, I'm not mad.

But what happened yesterday has got me extremely shaken, stirred and confused.

I actually keep saying to myself, 'What the fuck for fuck's

sake?'

Oh, if you aren't sure what's going on, well let me give you the fucking 411.

My SISTER, my own flesh and blood, fucked Andre. Or at least I think she did. I don't know, she locked my OWN FUCKING BEDROOM DOOR.

There is so much I am pissed about right now.

I'm at work and absolutely nothing is getting done. To be honest, I didn't come here to actually do work. I needed to be out of my place. First of all, Brina is a... oooo... I know it's blood over bollocks at all times but it's hard. These particular pair of bollocks belong to me and there is nothing I'm doing for him that any other woman out there can do better. The way he makes me feel about myself, I feel like I can walk on water sometimes. Like I get giddy and shit just thinking about him smiling at me.

Anyway, anyway, anyway... So, Brina came round to see me after I was M.I.A. for the *Black Panther* premier, which looked beautiful on my Instagram by the way. I missed a fucking moment with that one. But she didn't come round or call first or knock on my door, no, she used her fucking emergency key and walked her tiny, midget self up into my house, probably watched me and Andre sleeping and waited for me to wake up in the dark like some Bond villain. Then she carried on the shit Russia and Katrina started when it came to me and my enjoyment of Andre's excellent penis. Their 'dickmatised' theory. Which I still think is bollocks by the way. Like, I at least understand HOW someone could get addicted to a dick but I still don't think I'm there yet.

Well my bitch sister thinks I am. And she decided to fucking test me. Being my sister, she knew exactly what to say and how to say it in order to rile me up and it worked. She talked me into a trap where anything I said would've sounded like the fourth stages of intense dick addiction. Now I know some of you are thinking: why didn't you just tell her the truth, well what is the truth?

Do YOU think I'm addickted to Andre?

No, be honest. Looking at everything so far, do you think he's hooked me?

Okay, I mean, missing *Black Panther* was quite big because I was so hype for that film but other than that... nothing else I don't think.

So anyway... you know what? You already know what happened, you just read it. And to be honest, I don't even wanna talk about it because I'm so angry and annoyed and irritated and horny.

And the worst thing... the thing that made it all worse?

By the time I got out of the shower, they were both fucking gone! My bedroom door was now unlocked and I charged in like I was there to collect a debt.

Sniffing the air instantly, I couldn't tell if the sex scents in the air were from what we did the night before or what she did to him. And neither of them were answering their phones either so I couldn't get any answers from any fucking one.

And remember, that was in the morning. It's early evening the next day and I've STILL not heard from either of them. Andre hasn't been online since his last message from the day before and Brina was strangely quiet and not engaging in Russia and Katrina's *Black Panther* hype messages in the group.

So, technically, TECHNICALLY, I don't know if Brina and Andre had sex but... can I be honest with you? The way I felt walking into my bedroom and seeing my freshly made bed with new sheets with no-one in them made me break down. The not knowing, the wondering. One of them even went as far as to put my old sheets in the washing machine so I couldn't give them a thorough sniffing investigation. Then again, that may not have pulled up much. I came a LOT on those sheets too.

When I say I broke down, I sat on my bed and burst into tears. Not like a tear thinking about my dead dog from when I was five, I'm talking about tears streaming, bogey running, curled up in the foetal on my bed like a fucking baby type crying. Oh my God...

I stayed there in that position so long, I fell asleep and woke up the next damn day. That's today. Woke up and jumped off my bed like it was lava, imagining my sister and her little short, sturdy, midget-self on top of Andre and running her hands through her dry-ass, crispy relaxed hair with her fucking split ends.

That was the moment I had to get out of there so here I am at work, listening to SiR's *Liberation* featuring Anderson .Paak with my shoes off and my feet on my desk, watching YomsTV videos on Instagram.

He usually tickled me in a next way but he wasn't having the desired effect. Was that a sign?

I had a moment earlier on where I thought about something Brina said to me yesterday that has annoyingly stayed in my head.

'You ARE dickmatised baby sister. You are... You're place isn't looking as spotless as it usually is!'

OoOoOoOooo... that burned me more than a little bit. My PLACE isn't looking as spotless? Not looking AS spotless mah G?! Are you fucking kidding me? She somehow thinks that dick has affected my ability to clean!? What did she even mean 'not looking as spotless'? I haven't even taken you to her house about she's talking about spotless. My girl's got plaster falling off her walls and she's got bare, unvarnished wood floors... who is she to try and talk to me about spotless?

The way she said 'you ARE dickmatised' like it's something spiritual that happened without me realising. She all grabbed me by the shoulders like she was trying to shake some sense into me.

My phone was spinning between my fingers but I was not checking on any message from Andre. I wasn't checking them but that didn't mean I wasn't thinking about if he sent one or not. I'd created a shortcut on my phone's home screen that took me straight to his messages but I didn't check them. I just kept spinning my phone between my fingers. Musically, I was in an Anderson .Paak's *The City* kind of mood.

I didn't know what to do with myself. Yeah there was 101 things I could do to help with the alleged premier of our, no MY, Tatiana Blue documentary. I say alleged because apparently someone got a Russell Reed interview that may or may not have made the final cut so the premier in our office was alleged.

But I didn't want to do fuck all.

I just wanted to...

My phone vibrated between my fingers and I looked up at the giant wall calendar we had marked with notes, dates, times and address locations . Following the days, I stopped at the 14th.

'Valentines fucking day... for fuck's sake Andre...'

Kicking my legs off my chair, I spun around, trailing my legs so I went round for as long as I could. 'What the fuck are you doing to me MANUUUUUUH?'

I mean, even my condom drawer was open. Sorry to go back but I've just remembered something about when I went in my bedroom and Brina and Andre were gone. My condom drawer was half open but I didn't find a used condom or wrapper anywhere. Maybe she didn't use one.

'SHE FUCKING WOULDN'T!'

The hypocrisy was NOT lost on me, okay?

My phone lit up in my spinning grip and I saw Andre's name flash across my notifications. My feet stopped the spinning and I brought my knees up to my chest, opening the message with a heavy sigh.

'The fuck Andre,' I said for no reason.

Andr3: Are you busy tonight? I'd really like to talk.

TALK!?!

About what? What does HE want to talk to me about? It better be an explanation as to what the FUCK he did with my sister in the same bed he fucked me in hours before.

Even though I wanted those answers, I still wanted to just see him. Have a moment where I cum and he holds me through it, letting me go when it passes.

Question: every time I talk about Andre, do I talk about sex? I'm just asking.

Anyway, what did he want to talk about?

$imone: What the fuck do you want to talk about? Is it about how you fucked my sister RAW in my fucking bed? What were you thinking you nasty piece of shit?

I deleted that.

There were several return arguments he could throw at me: WE fucked without protection so who was I to talk and, secondly, I fucking told my sister to go and do it.

$imone: No, I want to talk to YOU. Don't you think you owe me some kind of fucking explanation? No? Maybe not?

I liked this one but I still deleted it.

$imone: You know what Andre? I can't do this anymore... I think we shou...

I deleted this one so quick, I tried to pretend I never even thought of it. That was like my rash, fuck it thinking coming through. I didn't want to spend any more time thinking about life without Andre's dick in my life so I went for cool and calm.

$imone: What's up?

Andr3: We need to talk about something and it's not something we can talk about on the phone or thru messages. Can I pass round later on?

$imone: You think my name is Pat Butcher? Lik I'm some lonely bitch sitting at home waiting for you? You think you can just come back to my place after...

Delete.

$imone: Sure... come around 9ish.

And with that, he was gone. He didn't even reply to say he was in the agreement with the time. My nerves were shot. I was still staring at my phone and I leaned all the way back in my chair and spun around with a highly frustrated groan.

'WHAT THE FUCK ANDRE?'

My usual excitement - and wetness - at the mere thought of seeing him was doused as there was something he wanted to talk about. Everyone has either said it or heard it before in a relationship at one point in their life. And the time between hearing it and having the actual conversation is the shit that burns. Because now, I've got...

'Six hours...'

Six hours until we have this talk. What am I gonna fucking do?

'Well I'm not doing work...'

I scooped up my keys, laptop and a few folders to read at home and I made my way home to start cleaning.

Apparently I wasn't representing the standard of cleanliness and excellence my late mother set in an amazing career in interior design.

About... my place isn't looking as spotless as it usually is!

Yeah that one's gonna piss me off all the way home.

Choosing a random grime playlist from Spotify, I got into my pre-ordered cab and closed my eyes all the way home. I needed some real deal Holyfield music that will totally make me forget about what I was failing to stop thinking about.

At one point in the back of the cab, I rubbed my legs together and heard my pussy lips squelch so loud, I had to look up to make sure the cab driver didn't hear it. Yeah, it was THAT fucking loud. Rode the rest of the way home with my hands between my legs.

Once inside, I threw everything on my spot on the sofa, got my gloves on, pulled out my basket of cleaning products and looked around, wondering where to start first.

'Oh, that's the bedroom FOR sure!'

I kept my headphones in, enjoying the bass in my ears as I pulled off the sheets that my sister or Andre put on my bed, haphazardly by the way. The ends of the duvet cover weren't clipped properly, the duvet wasn't properly inside...

By the time I got to Drake and Giggs on *KMT*, I had blitzed through my bedroom, spanked the living room and had the kitchen smelling all clinical, smelling all bleachy. UMMMMM!

Checking my watch, I'd lost more than four hours cleaning. That happens sometimes. Put some music on, take my basket and just clean. It's therapeutic. Something mum used to say.

I gave my battery a check and, on my notifications bar, I saw Andre's name. That made me rush to the message.

Before reading it, I caught myself with my shoulders hunched over and I was holding the phone with both hands like I was going to drop it. I relaxed, switched my weight to one leg and exhaled with an air of easy and breezy to it.

Andr3: I finished work early so I'm having a coffee at the cafe across the road from your place. I'm ready when you are.

He was fucking early. According to 9ish, that meant any time from 9pm onwards, not...

'An hour and fifteen minutes early... what the fuck?'

Looking myself up and down, I wasn't dressed for how I wanted to receive him for this 'talk'. Oh don't think the talk left my mind... but that's the other thing my mum taught me about cleaning. It has a way of helping you think about your problems in an order that makes the problem easy to clean. Never used to understand that as a child but I get it now.

She would love to hear me say that right now.

Into the living room to light an incense stick, next into the bathroom to run the shower.

I was going to make him wait... I wasn't going to be hanging on his every second. Not after what he did with Brina.

He was going to have to earn me back.

The shower was a quick one, the greasing even quicker and I was back in the living room in my loose but tight bed shorts and Wu Tang Chocolate Deluxe t-shirt and slippers sending him a message telling him to come up. I started to walk to the bedroom to get a piece of material to wrap my hair then stopped and went to the kitchen to boil the kettle for a mocha then I reached for my phone to play music.

I stopped and raised my hands to myself.

'Okay, relax yourself... what's wrong with you?'

My heart was beating as I pictured every step Andre was taking from the fancy coffee shop across the road from my block of overpriced apartments. Crossing the road, looking left and right and scaling the two steps before pressing my...

The sound of my intercom broke me from my calming session and I ordered my thoughts. I moved to the kitchen first and boiled a fresh pot of water, played Syd's *Insecurities* through my speaker and picked a piece of material I had hanging on the back of my bathroom door. All while the intercom continued to ring.

My breathing got heavy with each step I took towards my intercom phone. I tied my hair up so my face had a regal air. I was ready for whatever the fuck Andre wanted to talk about.

I was still nervous though.

Picking up the phone with a shaky hand...

'Hello?'

'It's me,' he said and I closed my eyes and inhaled with a thirsty smile.

'Come up.'

Buzzing him in, I hung up the phone, wiggling my hand to get rid of whatever that shaky shit was. I unlatched the door slowly with my head on the door.

'Oh yeah, incense...'

Lighter, stick, holder...

I fanned it with my hand so it smelled like I'd been burning it for a long time, not just for his arrival.

'OoOo, let's be in the kitchen and be like "I'm in the kitchen come on in". Yeah all cool, calm and collected.'

Skipping to the kitchen, knowing he would be at the door

any moment, I got a cup out. Then two. Then I put one back.

'He can damn well ask me for a drink.'

I pulled out a jar of Kenco coffee and Options Chocolate orange coco powder and two sachets of brown sugar. Two spoons of coffee, three of chocolate, sachet and a half of sugar and milk. Mix thoroughly and wait for the hot water.

Three raps knocked on my door.

My head turned quick as fuck.

I cleared my throat. 'I'M IN THE LIVING KITCHEN!'

The living kitchen you know? What the fuck was wrong with me? Ruined my whole sexy, 'I don't care' thing.

I went back to mixing my paste of flavours, digging the bottom of the cup for hidden pockets of mixture that usually floated up afterwards. Eugh.

My front door opened. I felt it. My toes curled in my slippers but I forced them straight.

The door closed and slow footsteps walked through my corridor.

As if on perfect cue, Barbara Streisand and Barry Gibbs's *Guilty* started and I laughed so hard, I slapped the counter as the kettle boiled.

'I'm in the KITCHEN!' I made sure I said it word perfect this time.

The door to the living room opened and the slow footsteps continued towards me. Out of fucking nowhere I had a fantasy about Andre pretending to be someone who broke into my apartment, couldn't find anything worth taking so he takes it out on me. Like full bally over faces, tie me up, take me even though I'm saying no type fantasy.

THAT one was definitely new!

I was properly taken aback for a second.

Then I felt the eyes on me from behind. My back straightened to give him the best view of my shape. The shorts flowed loosely over my hips but cinches at the waist and my t-shirt only reached just below my underboob.

He started walking towards me. I felt him moving. It was as if I was floating out of my body and was watching him watching me. At that exact moment, I wanted him to push me forward, pull my shorts down, spit on his dick and slide into me. That urge started to scream the closer he got. And he still hadn't said a word. Which made my chest start heaving.

Reaching for the kettle with my hand on full-blown Parkinsons, I poured the hot water slowly, battling the urge to turn around and look at him. I didn't want to give him the satisfaction of saying something first but I sooooo wanted to hear his voice.

'Hello Andre.'

Awww for fuck's sake!

He took a step right behind me then another and the hairs on the back of my neck stood up. He STILL hadn't said a word and I was squirming while my clit started to throb of its own accord.

Fuck, this man had a command over my body and he hadn't even touched me or said anything.

His arms slid under mine onto the counter and his torso came in contact with my back. I was glad he couldn't see my face because my eyes rolled in the back of my head and I was mouthing the words: for fuck's sake what are you doing to me boy? Are you kidding me right now? Oh my God...

His head rested on the back of my neck and he exhaled tiredly and I wanted to do nothing but turn around, wrap my arms around him and tell him everything was going to be alright. The way he let the air out of his lungs said that something was up.

With my drink mixed, I slipped my hands along his arms and wrapped them around my waist. The sound he made... SWEET JESUS!!!

Who the fuck is this guy? He's killing me right now... ARRRRGHHH!!!!

His arms squeezed me and his waist wiggled against me. My hands reached back and stroked the back of his neck. His lips kissed the back of my neck. My own hum escaped from the hidden depths of my soul. He got hard very quickly behind me. I adjusted my stance so he grew between my cheeks. He trailed one hand down over the front of my shorts. My head fell back against his shoulder. He was breathing heavily and hungrily in my ear. I was breathing in because it's like he was making the air suck out of my body. His other hand reached up and slipped under my t-shirt. I couldn't breathe. He exhaled in my ear. I let out the longest breath and felt my clit throbbing and a lot of instant wetness between my thighs.

'I wanted to come here and talk to you... I didn't MEAN to start this,' he said breathlessly in my ear.

Oh my gOd... I shivered and purred and came and tried to say words all at the same time. All I could do was hold onto the counter and leave my head back on his shoulder.

He needs to not talk again... ever!

I'm sorry T'Challa, you're the shit and all but this black panther of mine can rule me any time!

Has he really got me forsaking the king?

For fuck's sake!

Monday 12th February 2018

Awake slowly found me and tiredness hit me straight after. My eyes blinked open and a lick of light from the window hit me straight in the eye. I tried to block it with my arm but it was wrapped around Andre's neck. Looked like I was choking him in his sleep.

How I don't know. I let him go and started to get up, at least to find out what time it was but I stopped. I got stuck staring at him. Laying on his back with his arms perfectly by his side, his chest rising and falling, just peaceful. Unlike me last night.

Erm, but did we talk though? Fuck no... I didn't even get to drink my hot drink. From the time he had me squirting on my bleachy floor, there was no time for talk. Yeah I still wanted answers but I'd cum like three times before he even reached for my shorts.

He was hungry Andre. Hungry Andre growls a lot. THAT shit turns me on like you wouldn't believe. Are you joking? Hungry, handsome black man growling while he devours his meal? Prize number one. I was offering myself to him like a waitress and everything on the menu was his for the taking.

Yet again, we blessed every room in my place, went back against the window, this time me getting the head and he did this thing with my shower head, my waterproof bullet and his index finger I can't even physically describe.

There he was... just sleeping.

I was happy.

Not SO happy because we were sleeping in the same bed he fucked my sister in. Apparently. I still have to say apparently because I don't KNOW that anything happened. Although I still couldn't get Brina on the phone.

A 'gurummmmm' sound escaped from his lips and I leaned my head on my hand and watched him sleep. Memories of the way he wondered at my body deep into the early hours of the morning like a man possessed flooded my mind and my shoulders rolled.

How many of you reading this think Andre should be my boyfriend? Show of hands. Of course I've thought about it. I mean look at him. He's handsome as fuck. He's so handsome he's almost pretty. Look at those cheekbones, perfect nose, sexy, well kept beard, lips that do the fucking MOST, tongue that...

I sighed happily.

No but, seriously, why wouldn't Andre want to be my boyfriend? I mean I'm a strong black woman, doing my thing, working, got my own place, going places professionally, great in bed, clever, funny as hell I think, gym regularly, sexy in a pair of heels, understanding... what's not to like? Who wouldn't want to hold me closer than close?

There have been times after we've had sex and we've been staring at each other and talking about random shit where I've wanted to ask him about us being a couple but he's never given me any indication that that's what he wanted this to be.

Yeah I could ask but I didn't want to ask and he says no

and then not only do I have to deal with that rejection but then he also takes the dick away from me too.

Nah, I'm alright thanks.

But we'd make a good couple I think. There's actually a few things I think we could collaborate on which could help bring in some extra money. Maybe we could find a two-bedroom somewhere in Doncaster. I heard prices are going down in that area in 2018. With my salary and his computer thing, we could be doing alright for ourselves. I can get him into playing Badminton with me and we can argue over who's cooking dinner. If he doesn't eat or know about jollof though, we might have to rethink this whole thing because I can't be with a man who doesn't like jollof. That's sacrilege. I mean who doesn't like jollof rice? Andre does, I can tell. No man can do the things he does with his tongue and not like jollof rice. I wonder if I could find a good caterer who could do jollof at a good price. Maybe get someone's aunt to make some rice and peas. I wonder if Andre would agree to letting us get married in a castle. I could be like a real fucking princess... no a QUEEN in a castle. Oh that's the dream right there. I imagine he'd be all practical and say, 'yeah but people are gonna be cold in a castle'. But it's not about them, it's about me... and him of course. Long as he doesn't suggest some *Don't Tell The Bride* nonsense then I'm cool. I wouldn't care what kind of wedding we had. Although I'm not turning up in no fucking field in my sexy as fuck wedding dress. No way. If not a castle then a church that looks like a medieval castle with long bits and dark bits and an echo inside. So when Andre tells me he does, I want everyone to hear it. I want it to reverberate against every and any ear in the church, into God's ear and to all the other women out there that Andre is taken. He is mine. This dick right here belongs to me. I am not, in any way, shape or form, letting this man go for some peppercorn neck-back rat bag to get this good dick? Nuh suh, nuh uhh. If it has to be sloppy then sloppy it is, if its fuck my face then face fucking it is. But I am not letting anyone touch him. How can this chocolate divine being, this beautiful providence, this supernatural force, this MAN... how can he be anything else but mine? You tell me!

While I'm waiting, I'm gonna snuggle up to this Divine Being and go back to sleep. Wiggling under his arm, I laid on his shoulder not taking my eyes off his sleeping face. I wondered what he was dreaming about and if I was anywhere in his dream? Did he dream? Not everyone did and most people forget them by the time they woke up. As eloquent as Andre can be, he could tell me I was riding a unicorn backwards holding a plate of sausage rolls singing *I Will Survive* in his dream but fuck me, I'd listen.

I am NOT addicted!

Tuesday 13th February 2018

'The FUCCCK...' I said out of my sleep.

With a frown and a meerkat pose, I was laying on my stomach with my arms holding me up thinking that something felt wrong. Andre was gone. But I hadn't fully woken up so I wasn't sure if my eyes were playing tricks on me or not.

I itched my booty and shook my head.

Yep, he was gone.

But that was the other thing that was wrong.

He was gone but I could smell something. A sweet warm smell that was drifting in light and heavy waves. I took a full whiff and separated pancakes from sausages and something else with a sweetish cinnamon flavour.

And coffee. Fresh coffee.

Oh I was awake now.

Draping my dressing gown over my naked body, *Adventure Time* slippers on my feet, I went to see what was going on.

Hope was secretly bubbling in my stomach.

Musiq's *Previouscats* was playing low through my speakers and the kitchen light gave the living room an eerie, 'there's shit going on in here' glow. With the curtains still closed, I leaned around the door from the living room, trying to see something before he noticed I was there. My steps were quiet but I was enjoying the smells I was picking up. Still couldn't place the cinnamon scent that was making my stomach grumble though.

'Hungry?' Andre said without looking at me.

'How did you know I was...'

'I've picked you up and fucked you against your window. I know what you sound like on your feet.'

'Who are you *Mcgyver*?'

'Fuck *Mcgyver*. He didn't have shit on Hannibal and the boys.'

I came round the door into the kitchen and I had to stop.

In fact, I rushed back to the bedroom and got my phone and got my camera up then came back. Video on and... record.

Andre was in my petite kitchen and he was doing the most. I could see a plate of pancakes that he added another one to, he was stirring something and checking something in my oven. And he was as naked as the day God made him.

'Aren't you worried about anything... you know... spattering?'

'When you know what you're doing, you know what to fear and what not to fear.'

He laughed. I scoffed and snorted because it caught me by surprise.

'So,' I started, ready to move past the fact that I SNORTED as a grown-ass woman. 'What you doing in here?'

'Erm... sorry you can't be in here.'

He turned around quickly and his dick swung back and forth for a few seconds after. I was mesmerised. I brought the phone down to watch him swing and he wasn't even hard.

'Are you kicking me out of my own kitchen?'

'Yes,' he replied looking at and through me.

'Are you serious?'

'Yes I am.'

He walked towards me and closed the space between us real quick and the air sucked out of my lungs. Jill Scott's *Crown Royal* played from the living room.

'Lemme just see what you're making and...'

Andre put his hands under my arms and lifted me out of the kitchen while I was trying to look at what was going on behind him.

'You are banned from the kitchen young lady.'

My legs wrapped behind him instinctively. Every time he picked me up that's what I did so why should now be any different? I locked around his waist and he put his arms around me and walked us into the living room.

'OoOoOooo Melvin!' I said seductively.

He stopped. 'Did you just call me someone else's name?'

'Melvin. From *Baby Boy*. Ving Rhames character? Big naked black man cooking naked in the kitchen and drinking all the juice and fucking Tyrese's mum while he was sleeping in the next room?'

'Oh yeaaaaaah...'

He put me down softly on the sofa in my spot as Childish Gambino's *Redbone* started and, I swear to you, this moment couldn't of been any sexier. He kissed me on my forehead, wiggled his dick and walked off back to the kitchen. Leaning back, folding my legs under me and getting comfortable, I brought my still recording phone up and turned the light on. I didn't care if he saw me. We made worse videos last night against the window. He had me literally climbing the walls last night. At one point I was trying to scale my bed frame and get away from him because he refused to let go of my thighs and let me have an orgasm in peace. He was eating my pussy with delicious ferocity as he always does and he set off a chain of orgasms that doubled every time he licked my clit. But instead of letting the orgasm have it's moment, he troubled it by licking my clit WHILE I was having the orgasm which set off another one. And another one and another one. They were starting before the last one finished. Overlapping and jumping over each other trying to get out first. Meanwhile I'm flapping around throwing pillows off the bed, scratching his back trying to get out of his grip but he wouldn't let me go. I was literally climbing the walls and I know because I stopped for a second and pictured just what the fuck I was doing.

Oh God... this man!

'Can I ask questions about the food?'

'Hmmm... yes or no questions only. Go.'

He started chopping something and his strong man-cheeks started to shake. I shook with him and grumbled under my breath. 'Yeaaaaaaaaaah... shake it!'

'Are there pancakes?'

'Yes.'

'What else?'

'No.'

'What you mean no?' I asked, stretching my legs. Lots my random bruises that I couldn't understand because I don't remember hurting myself.

I forgot my phone was recording and turned it off.

'That's not a yes or no question.'

'Oh for fuck's sake... okay. Is there something to accompany the pancakes?'

'Yes.'

'Is there more than one thing to accompany the pancakes?'

'Yes.'

Oooo, I was enjoying this game. Mainly because I was getting yes answers. And which woman ever wants to hear the word no?

'Does dick come with that breakfast?'

'Dick comes without breakfast. Yes or no questions lady!'

'Okay, okay, okay... erm... will I be full after breakfast?'

He mixed something and he wiggled again. I shimmed my shoulders with him.

'Definitely.'

'Will I want to eat, have a nap, wake up and fuck you then go back to sleep again?'

This question carried a bit more weight to it because I wanted to know what he was doing for the rest of the day. Maybe even find out if he was free tomorrow. Not that he HAD to be free for me but... yeah he had to be free for me tomorrow. He is not gonna eat my pussy in front of night-time London with my phone on a selfie-stick balanced between two cushions, making us look like a fucking movie and not be free for me on Valentines Day.

Yeah, he did that last night.

'Madam, after this, you'll want to eat, sleep, wake up, finish the rest, have round... what are we on?'

'Are you even trying to keep count?'

'Round whatever, wake up again, fuck my face, sleep AGAIN, wake up tomorrow and do it all over again.'

Wait!? Is it me or does that sound like he just made a plan with me for Valentines Day? He said: fuck my face... yeah I remembered from the important point. He said: fuck my face, sleep AGAIN, wake up tomorrow... Now that's the important part. Because today is today. Today is Tuesday the 13th of February. So by him saying 'wake up tomorrow' that means he wants to wake up with me on Valentines Day, right? I'm not going mad or over-reading into something that isn't there am I? Me and my "dickmatised" self isn't reaching for hope here am I?

I needed a clearer answer.

'So does that mean...'

'Is this gonna be a yes or no question?'

GOD! Even just bantering with this man has got me

thinking about the arguments we'll have about what to name our kids. He doesn't look like someone of the opinion that champagne brands and sports cars are suitable names for children. I was going to have to find a way to sneak that one into a random conversation. And we did those. A lot. The maddest, most random conversations you can't even explain afterwards. You just had to be there. Okay, here's an example. Have you ever seen a film called *Predestination*? 2014 time travelling film with Ethan Hawke in a mad storyline that I couldn't explain if I tried but it made us have a two-hour point-to-point conversation about a question that the film made us ask each other. The question was: if you had a sex change and then became a time traveller, would you go back in time and fuck yourself? Yeah, exactly... what a mad question and yet, for two hours, we debated back and forth about why that was so messed up. Andre was of a different opinion and believed it would be okay to do so because the you of the past could really need a lay at that precise moment. He also added that being a woman would allow him to remember what it was he likes, thus it'd be a pretty easy lay. A win-win for everyone. I tried to introduce the space time-continuum and how if you step on a snail in the past, it'll have an effect in the future. That went onto *Groundhog Day, The Butterfly Effect, Memento, 12 Monkeys,* even *Bill and Ted's Excellent Adventure*. In the end, we fell asleep without resolving it. Well he fell asleep, I watched him sleep for a few hours.

'Any more questions before breakfast is served? And I should warn you, I've made a healthy portion.'

'Isn't it cheat day?' I asked playfully.

'It IS cheat day,' he replied with a giggle.

I died inside just a little bit.

Oh yeah, Valentines.

'So you feel like waking up with me on Valentines day do you?'

He turned his head to the side. 'There's nowhere else to be Miss Climb-The-Walls-Monkey-Style.'

'Don't you dare even think about talking about that EVER again.'

He spun around - his dick did that thing again - and wielded a spatula at me.

'Did you or did you not agree to the forfeit?'

'You gave me...'

'Yes or no? Did you or did you not agree to the forfeit? In fact, let's get it all on the table. Why did you have a forfeit in the first place?'

I heard him but my eyes were interested in his dick, the way it just hung there, all beautiful and... siiiiiiiiiiiiiiigh.

He must've noticed my head tilt to the side because he did the same to get my attention.

'I'm sorry, what did you say?'

'Yeah, eyes up here! Why were you given a forfeit in the first place? Remember we were both there.'

'Because...'

'Speak up,' he laughed. 'They can't hear you in the back!'

'Because I came first in a 69!'

'One more time for the Uckers in the back?'

He leaned closer holding the spatula like a microphone.

I reached out to playfully slap him and he went into a kung-fu dance.

Again, I was watching but my eyes just... Kept. Drifting. To. His. Dick.

Every time it bounced or moved or grew, I just wanted to hug it and tie a bow around it and take selfies with it.

'I lost a 69 competition! I came first.'

'YES SHE DID LADIES AND GENTLEMEN, SHE CAME FIRST. USUALLY A GOOD THING BUT IN THIS COMPETITION NOT SO MUCH!'

I felt like I was looking up at a deity as he looked down from his imaginary crowd, grabbed my hand, kissed it and bounced back into the kitchen.

Carry on and see if I stop you from pulling out next time.

Fuck me, wash my thoughts out!

Where are these random-ass thoughts coming from? We've been close a few times. Sometimes, when he says he's about to cum, I swear I've almost said: cum in me. Just because I've wanted to feel him let go completely with me. I've got the coil in so I'm not worried about getting pregnant. Although, a baby with my eyes and his facial bone-structure would be GORGEOUS. His eyebrows and my lips, his chocolate highlight and my nose? Oh wow.

'Okay, you are responsible for finding us something to watch because breakfast is served.'

Reaching from the remote while leaning to watch him scrape something from a frying pan onto a plate that looked like it had a lot of food, I groaned at his behind.

I turned on my Sky Q and went straight to movies-on-demand.

'Have you seen *Get Out* yet?' I asked, moving to my planner.

'No I haven't! SO many people have told me to watch it and they've told me how good it is but I don't know. The guy from Key and Peele is funny but I don't know how good he'll be at doing a horror film.'

OKAY, MIND MERGE MOMENT RIGHT HERE!

That's exactly why I hadn't seen it either. That exact same reason. I loved Key and Peele and I loved *Keanu* because it was them doing their funny thing but horror? I wasn't sure.

Fuck me, the exactly same thought.

'Me neither. People have hyped it up so much, I don't want to watch it and end up disappointed.'

Inside I was screaming: WE THINK THE SAME THING ABOUT THE SAME FILM... YAAAAAAAY!

His head appeared from the kitchen. 'Wanna be disappointed together?'

'I'm up if you're down,' I replied with a relationship smile.

The rest of his body followed and, ladies and gentleman, the boy made me one heck of a breakfast. My stomach suddenly rumbled like I was starving her on purpose.

'What the hell have you done here?'

I didn't know where to look. He'd put my plate of food on a fold-out tray with legs so I could sit back in my spot.

'This is breakfast. Cinnamon and mixed spice pancakes, asparagus and spring onion scrambled eggs, vegan sausage meat and waffles with a light drizzle of melted icing sugar sprinkled on top. AND, fresh Ethopian Harrar coffee.'

I put my hands up - watching his dick dangle as he lent towards me - and was happily assaulted by the different flavours.

'Oh shit, I forgot syrup, hold on...'

My hands were still up in surrender, looking down at everything trying to remember what it all was. All I remembered was vegan sausage meat and something from Ethiopia. It all looked sooooo good and I was suddenly sooo hungry for it. Mainly because he made it for me in my own kitchen... naked.

'Ethopian coffee? And you made that using MY kettle?'

'No, I went home and got my coffee machine. It's made especially for this particular kind of coffee.'

'When did you go home?'

'When you were dead to the world after trying to climb the walls.'

'Are you serious?'

He appeared from the kitchen from the with a jar of Hilltop Boilers Pure Maine Maple Syrup and his own tray of food. 'Yeah, I brought my waffle-maker too.'

'YOU own a waffle-maker?'

'Is it so strange for a black man to own a waffle-maker?'

Not strange, just something I've never thought of before.

'Not strange just... I don't know. You never think of black men and waffle-makers in the same sentence. It's not a sentence you say everyday put it that way.'

He nodded his head. 'I'll give you that one.'

Sitting softly next to me - still as naked and beautiful as the day he was born - Andre put his cup on the table. He'd laid out a black dressing gown that must've been his. He took my cup of coffee off my tray and put it on the table in front of us.

'...so you don't spill it...' he mumbled.

My eyes hadn't left him since he walked in the with the

syrup and sat down. It was nice that he cared if I spilled my drink or not. I'm hoping my face didn't look like some lovestruck, chupid schoolgirl with a crush on the new guy in class.

'Thanks,' I said.

He was opening the syrup in the darkness of the room, fighting to get the plastic wrapper off the lid. He began scratching and gnawing at it and it was a giggle to watch him go at it.

I took it from him softly, held up my middle finger and ran it along the base of the lid. My nail cut through the plastic and it fell away from the lid and I fluttered fast eyebrows while handing the bottle back to him.

Wednesday 14th February 2018 (1)

Valentines day!

What a fucked up time of year. Different for so many people. The absolute shit if you've got someone and if you don't, a nasty, vicious reminder that no-one wants you. Even on the day where everyone is supposed to want someone. Then again, I know some women in relationships who still have shit Valentines.

For the past three years, I've spent Valentines Day alone. Not by choice, it just always seems to work out that way. One relationship ended two days before and tried to come back three days later.

But fuck me for fuck's sake... that's changed this year.

I've been up for about an hour. Yes, again, watching him sleep.

For about 20 minutes of that hour, I wanted to sit on his face and smother the shit out of him. Just because he was there and I could.

Is there something wrong with that? Not smother him like kill him... just... you know so he has to hold his breath for a minute. Squash his nose but not break it, you know?

That's not bad is it?

Oh, this is killing me, I'm going back to sleep. Doze on these filthy thoughts I'm having.

Waking up suddenly again, I reached for my phone and checked the time. It was apparently 6pm. Which HAD to have been bullshit! There was no way it was that time. Where had the fucking day gone?

I looked left and right and Andre was gone.

'Andre?'

Nothing.

There were no smells to adjust my nose to or sizzling sounds coming from my kitchen. No music playing from the living room.

Where was my Andre?

Did he actually fucking leave me? No he couldn't have.

He promised - well he didn't promise - but he said he was going to stay with me for Valentines. He said so.

Oh he better be in the shower but I couldn't hear any water running.

I jumped up without being fully awake and stumbled to my bedroom door. I threw my dressing gown over nothing but an X-Men t-shirt and held myself against the door frame.

I was on the cusp of screaming out 'ANDRE WHERE ARE YOOOOOU?' when he opened the bathroom door and steam billowed around him, making him look like an omnipotent spirit here to bless his willing subject with dick game, head game and enough random conversation and caring moments to put a ring on it.

Yeah, I've figured out that it's the dick that is making me say and think these random things that usually would have no place coming out of my mouth. Andre's magnificent, excellent, tremendous, stands on its own, blessed chocolate dick.

Even at this point, I'm still mesmerised by it. I mean it just… siiiiiigh.

It's just swell!

Insert dream sequence involving Andre's dick here!

'Well… hello!' I said meaning it exactly how it came out. Stuttered, broken, in awe and… yeah.

Water was dripping down his shoulders, he had a towel wrapped tightly around his waist and he was drying behind his head so his bicep muscle was squeezing and flexing in my face. All wanting me to lick it and shit.

'Well hello Miss Thinks She Ain't Gonna Climb The Walls Anymore. Think you can fuck with the big boys yeah?'

'I didn't climb the wall!'

That doesn't mean it was any easier to take the abuse, that's all I can call it. The ABUSE that he put on my pussy and my poor, inflated clit. I couldn't sleep with my legs closed, it was that big.

This fucking guy!

'Happy Valentines Day,' he said leaning to kiss me on my cheek.

The steam wafting over me smelled manly and Lynx-ish and I loved it.

I grabbed his dick, which was making an imprint on the front of his towel.

'Happy Valentines to you Mr Man.'

'You going in the shower?' he asked as I stroked falling drops of water down his chest.

'Was thinking about it. Strangely I'm thinking of something else now.'

'What's that?'

You FUCKING me in the shower!'

'Well that's not a way to get clean is it?'

'Who said I wanted to be clean?'

He raised his eyebrows at me. 'Is that how you're going on?'

Grabbing the front roll of towel by his belly button, I pulled him with me back into the bathroom and kicked the door closed.

'No wait, we've...'

My lips on his shut him up!

Now, somewhere between my sixth and seventh orgasm, I heard a knock on the door. Andre heard it to because he took my leg off his shoulder and opened the shower curtain, grabbing a towel as he went.

By the time I noticed he was gone, he'd clean left the bathroom.

'What the...'

I turned off the shower and grabbed my own towel, confused as hell.

Why was Andre running to my front door like he lived here? Was he expecting something or someone? Either way he knew what was going on at my front door and I didn't.

Not cool.

I heard the door open then I heard a clitter-clatter that made me stop drying myself and pay attention. Shower cap in place this time.

'Erm Andre?'

'Yes babe?'

He called me babe, awww.

'Who is at the door?'

'Yeah thank you... No-one is at the door. Just me and you baby!'

'Andre, I know what I heard.'

'And Simone, I said what I said,' he said mockingly.

That made me chuckle and but I didn't stop quick drying myself because I NEEDED to know who he answered the door to. He opened it to someone, I heard him. Maybe it was Brina, who was still fucking ignoring my calls and messages.

Oh MY GOD!

I didn't tell you. Andre told me what happened that morning I thought Brina went in and fucked him in my bed.

She didn't. He told me everything.

So, what happened was, she went in there and he woke up and she locked the door and you know what she did? Actually it's probably worse in the long run. She sat down with the dude and proceeded to tell him to leave me alone because whatever he was doing to me was making me addicted to him. Yes, she fucking told the guy to leave me alone because I was getting hooked on him. Not have a crush on him or maybe in love with him. No, HOOKED on him. Like I'm not a grown-ass woman with a mind of her own who doesn't know what she's doing? She told him about the conversation we had beforehand and told him that I wanted to disprove her so much that I sent her into my room to have sex with him. I denied that. To give it all effect, my sister locked the door, took a condom out of the drawer and changed my sheets. Andre said he didn't want to stay for whatever my sister was doing and he left. He said he knocked on the bathroom before he left but I remember at that point I didn't want to hear anything that was going on outside of the steaming hot shower I was trying to melt in.

With my towel around my waist I opened the bathroom door just as Andre closed the living room door. We stood for a moment looking at each other.

'What was that?' I asked, my eye catching something before the door closed.

'What was what?'

'THAT... I just saw a wheel in my living room. Why is there a wheel in my living room?'

'Don't worry they're clean.'

'Oh THEY are? How many wheels are in there and what are they wheels on?'

'Could you go and put some clothes on please?'

'I'm not going any fucking where until you tell me...'

'Look woman, can you, for once, do as you're told and go and get dressed?'

He spun me round and spanked me to send me on my way. It was a heavy hand that landed perfectly on my right cheek and it made me whimper while looking back at him.

Of COURSE I like that shit. Got me moving with some pep in my step.

I spun around. 'What should I wea...'

'Just go and get dressed-uhhhhhhhh!'

'Okay, okay, I'm going.'

And going I was gone.

It must've been a record how fast I got dressed. There was no method to the clothes I put on. It ended up being my *I Am BLUE* t-shirt and leggings with my hair wrapped and I was back in the dark corridor where I kicked something and sucked air through my teeth.

'What the fuck was that?'

Turning the light on, I saw a big black duffle bag and I kicked it again. Sounded like Andre's waffle-maker.

Aww what? He can't be leaving... no way... aww don't say that!

He walked out into the corridor and closed the living room door behind him. He was wearing clothes this time. Looking all neat and tidy in trousers and shirt with his top button open.

'Are we gonna stand out here or am I gonna find out why there are wheels in my living room?'

He sighed. 'Okay, but before you go in there, I just wanted to say that...'

'Okay,' was my last word before I pushed past him and opened the living room door.

'OH FOR FUCK'S SAKE!!!'

THIS FUCKING GUY!

Roses everywhere! When I say everywhere I mean everywhere. On my sofa, around my TV, on my table, in every nook and cranny of my TV unit, in the kitchen, on the counter, in the sink. They were EVERYWHERE. I didn't know where to look. And they were multi-coloured roses too so imagine... hold on. Two, four, six...

Imagine... 14 colours of roses around your entire living room. And in the middle, somehow, sat two trolleys - with wheels - and large shiny cloche covers over them.

My hands were over my mouth, my eyes watered and I had to fan myself so he wouldn't see me fucking...

No, don't... don't do it. Oh fuck... too late.

A single tear began to run down my face but I wiped it extremely quick, fast and in a hurry so he wouldn't see it.

'What do you...'

I reached a finger behind me and shushed him so he stopped talking.

I wasn't ready to hear his voice yet. I was still taking it all in and trying not to cry at the same time. Which I was.

THIS GUY IS RIDICULOUS.

I mean when did he find the time to do all this? How did, no WHEN did he find the time to get all this in and done without me knowing?

Any questions that needed answers would have to wait but, for the moment, I could feel more tears ready to fall.

'For fuck's sake Andre,' I said into my hands.

His arms snuck around my waist and his face nuzzled my neck.

'Happy Valentines Day Miss Shivers When She Cums!'

I scoffed. Not in any negative way but it was redundant to say happy valentines day when you rose-bombed my living room and kitchen and got us something to eat under cloches.

Fancy pants.

'Can I talk ye...'

I ran my finger up and down his lips without looking at him . 'Shhhhhhhhhhh, shhhhhhhhh, shhhhhh, shhhhhh, shhh... not yet Andre, just.. not yet!'

'I just wanted to say happ...'

'What part of NOT YET don't you understand?'

I turned to face him and his happy face made my tears run like Jamaicans in a 100 meter dash. Oh he made me bawl out. I had to hide my face in his shoulder because I couldn't believe how much I was crying. And the reason I was crying. I felt like a right Rodney at the moment because if he asked why I was crying I'd have to say it's because I'm so happy. Which always seems like crap when I've heard it before.

He hugged me with a dip so my shoulders were level with his and I let the tears fall. There was no point trying to hide them... they were tears of joy. And it wasn't the first time I'd cried in front of him. Some of the orgasms he made me have came equipped with that uncontrollable reaction as well. He just never saw them.

'Oh yeah, and I got you a card too.'

He left our space, leaving me empty.

'A card too? Oh of course for fuck's sake!'

I hope my fuck's sake counter is still reading with me.

Not moving an inch, getting my camera ready to take a panoramic picture of all the flowers in my room, Andre returned with a card.

'Here you go. But you can't open it yet.'

'Why not?'

'After you eat.'

'And what are we eating?'

'Well sit down and I'll tell you Miss Simone.'

The trolleys were sitting where my centre table used to be but was now flat against my large windows. Chairs were set either side and Andre motioned with his arm for me to sit down.

I followed and sat down and he did the same on the other side.

'Okay,' he started. 'So I heard Levi Roots was doing a special delivery service to 10 lucky people and guess who one of them was?'

'You?' I said, having one of my "in awe" staring moments.

'No, us!'

'The guy that does the reggae reggae sauce?'

'Same one.'

'He does a delivery service?'

'He might! He's testing something out at the moment.'

Excitement and hunger were making the fat Monica in me dance.

'Good evening Miss McKenzie. I am your host, Andre, and I shall be feeding you, yes, FEEDING you delectable delights from far and wide across the Caribbean.'

'OoOoOoOo... tell me more!'

I folded my feet under me and drummed my hands on the cloche in front of me tingling all fucking over.

'Right,' he said producing a menu from nowhere. 'You ready?'

'I smell goodness. What you feeding me?'

'Shit, it's a lot. Okay madam... tonight you shall be... uh oh wait wait wait...'

He pulled out his phone and *Slam Dunk The Funk* by 5ive began to play. We both looked at each other like: this is not mood music.

He burst into laughter a split second before me but although I found it funny, I wanted to watch him find it funny.

The music stopped and he cleared his throat.

I was paying him all the attention I had in my account.

Two notes from a double bass struck my ears and my eyebrows raised. I knew this song and I waited for the following notes, recognising it instantly. In my mind, I added up why he would play that song, appreciated the fact that he knew such a song, tied the song in to everything we'd done before and came up with my own equation as to why Andre chose Al Green's *Simply Beautiful.*

'Okay, Miss Simone. Tonight, we have....'

He lifted my cloche for me... like my man should.

'We have grilled lamb and coconut from risotto from St Lucia, Magret de canard from Martinique, ackee and saltfish from Jamaica, Yuana from Curacao, Keshi Yena, also from Curacao, Yucca and goat from Dominica, stone oven chicken from the British Virgin Islands and crayfish in a honey, lemon and rum glaze.'

Each dish was on a separate saucer, giving just a taste of a delicacy from the islands. I was looking at EVERYTHING and it all looked so good. Steaming hot with wild random flavours drawing my attention every which way. I didn't hear the microwave and he couldn't have warmed all this food in my oven, got it back onto my plate and had this much food ready in the time I was in the shower.

My mouth was watering at each plate which came with a place card explaining what it was. Andre removed his cloche and revealed the same collection of small plates.

There was a double-team job being done by my nose nose and eyes, recognising most of the food but I read a few of the ones I didn't.

'What is Magret de Canard?' I picked up the card. 'Oh duck breast with honey, orange and thyme... interesting.'

'You think that's interesting,' Andre said staring at a card and pointing. 'That Yuana over there is stewed Iguana.'

'STEWED... eugh...'

But it still looked delicious. If he didn't tell me what it was, I would've let my mouth tell me how it tasted. I can be adventurous like that sometimes. A part of me still wanted to taste it.

'THIS has a lid on it.'

There was a yellow thing on a plate that looked like a pot with a lid that intrigued me because it was so small. We both grabbed for our corresponding cards and read at the same time.

'Gouda cheese...' I mumbled.

'...stuffed and baked with a spicy meat,' he finished.

We looked at each other at the same time and reached for the cheese lid. Sniffing deeply at the white streaks of spicy steam that rose up, I was hungrier than ever.

He stood up quickly. So quick that I jerked back, still with awe on my face. Unfolding a material napkin, he draped it across my lap and kissed the side of my head. The air of comfort I exhaled was epic lemme' tell you. My eyes closed and I smiled, not fully, just to myself. A meme I saw the other day popped into my head that said something like "forehead kisses are the work of the Devil and suck common sense from women all over the world, beware". Or something like that, I don't know. I'm not sure if that's true or not because I think I've still got my common sense. AND my place is SPOTLESS!

Nipples up, inner thighs wet.

'Dig… in.'

Man o'man I didn't know where to start. My knife and fork were wrapped in tissue and Andre was pouring a pink drink into one of my long glasses and I just stopped to take it all in. The resplendent, magnificent black man sitting across from me, the flowers all around my living room, the music, the food, the set up… all of it.

'What?' Andre said, catching me staring at him.

'What?!' I said, having nothing to say.

'Aren't you gonna eat?'

'I want to!'

His dreamy eyes looked up from a piece of chicken to me.

'Are you talking about food or me?'

I let my silence answer for me.

My smile said everything else!

Wednesday 14th February 2018 (2)

'FUCK'S SAKE!' I yelled out of my sleep.

I didn't even know I WAS asleep!

Taking note of my body, I felt I was curled up. The scent of flowers told me I was in the living room.

'ANDR…'

A clatter of plates stopped me and I sat up straight away.

My dream appeared over as my living room was right back to the way it was. The trolleys and chairs were gone, my table was back in the middle of the room and the flowers were gone.

I REALLY want to know how the fuck he's getting all this done and I'm not noticing it. I was sitting up, confused.

Shaking off a humongous bout of the itis, bulbous stomach keeping me down, I rubbed my eyes and yawned.

Andre was in the kitchen washing plates it sounded like.

'Hey lover, hey lover' I sang out loud.

Andre stuck his head out of the kitchen. *'This is more than a cruuuuush!'*

The back and forth we engaged in was irrefutable and impossible to NOT enjoy. Impossible to not wonder. This thing of ours has become a fuck because every time we do it, I think of Andre as MINE. My boyfriend. My partner, soulmate, my lover and friend, my confidant and dildo with a pulse, my daddy and my throne to sit on, my pillow when I sleep, my cheering section, my chef, my personal vagina caretaker forever and ever and ever.

Why not? Stranger things have happened, right?

Walking back into the room, drying his hands, Andre leaned against the door-frame and there was something on his face. His eyes were tasting me, rolling his hands on my neck and grabbing my ass like it was his. But his LOOK wasn't happy.

'How the hell did you get this place cleaned up and where are my beautiful flowers?'

'I've put them in vases in every room. So there's a vase in the bathroom, one in the bedroom, one in the kitchen and the big one behind the sofa.'

At the same time, we looked behind my sofa and he reached down and produced a large vase of colourful roses and put it on my table.

'I don't have that many vases though.'

'The flowers came with vases so they're yours to keep.'

FREE VASES!

It felt like fucking Christmas!

'Simone?'

'Andre… I need to tell you something.'

It is 2018 ladies and gentlemen and I was about to shoot my shot! Why the fuck not? I'm honestly at that stage where I was tired of doing this. At least tired of not knowing. Tired of looking at Andre like he was the love of… no… like he was a man I thought I could go places with. Yet here I am happy to sit here waiting for him to drop some dick on me like some side dish sitting on the menu waiting to be ordered. I wanted him, that was obvious. I still don't believe I'm dickmatised but if the dick came with him then I guess I'd have to take it. And I'd take it again and again and again.

'I'm leaving.'

'You're doing what!?!'

Oh every fucking sexy, dreamy thought I was having at that moment became shit in my head and I titled to the side.

'I tried to tell you the other day but, we didn't do a lot of talking that night. And there was no place to talk about it after that. It's work, they've…'

'Hold on, wait? You didn't just mean you're leaving here to go home and come back tomorrow. You're talking about LEAVING. Leaving ME?!'

'Leaving London. Just for six months.'

'For SIX MONTHS? WHERE THE FUCK ARE YOU GOING?'

My whole demeanour had changed. I was no longer tired, I was sitting back against my sofa with my arms folded and I was paying full attention.

I could hear my tone and volume but I didn't care. This better be a fucking joke! Where the fuck is he trying to go?

'Japan.'

'Asia?'

'No, Japan in Grimsby, of course Asia,' he smiled.

His levity attempt was noted but I wasn't biting. I was getting angrier by the second. The longer he stood there, the more I didn't think he was lying.

My voice was deadpan. 'Why are you going to Japan Andre?'

'My company is expanding into other markets and they want me to go to Japan. For some reason, they decided to FINALLY listen to me and let me update their network system over here and it's working better than ever. So now they're expanding, they want me to take the same network over there.'

I was just nodding, listening but not listening. Taking in the major plot points and trying to turn the fire inside down to a low simmer. I am FUCKING LIVID inside though because Andre isn't saying, 'nah, I'm only joking'.

'So for six months, they want me to go out there and literally build a whole new network as part of this big expansion.'

The most ignorant and possibly racist shit came to my head and I wasn't sure how he'd take it or how it would even come out. I know if I said ANYTHING, my tone would make it sound more messed up than it did in my head.

But... why would his company be sending him to Japan when that side of the world is known for technological advancements? Like you mean to tell me there isn't a dude named T'wan who could do exactly the same thing as Andre without needing to fly him out there for SIX FUCKING MONTHS?

Suddenly the flowery scent of the room was annoying and I needed a cup of tea. I jumped out of my seat and rushed past him. The need for a hot drink was massive and I didn't want him to see me start crying.

I slapped the kettle on, bringing my arms across my eyes roughly and sniffing softly.

'Come on Andre, please be fucking joking!' I was whispering to myself, closing my eyes tight and thinking. And over-thinking and thinking OVER my over-thinking.

How was he gonna just do this to me and on fucking Valentines day as well. Who does that? How long did he know and why am I only finding out now for fuck's sake? What does he think is gonna happen, I'm gonna keep fucking him until he goes? Not that I won't but it would kill me to know that every time I saw him was leading to the last time I was going to see him. How was I even here? When I woke up, it was laughter, good times and dick-watching with my man... I mean Andre. Now here I was planning our last few sessions together.

I realised I'd been very quiet since his last sentence.

'Okay,' I started weakly. 'So when are you leaving?'

My breathing was raggedy. I was trying so hard to hold back an outburst.

'That's the thing. I'm leaving tonight.'

'YOU FUCKIN...'

My feet started to spin me around but I paused and gave him my back to stare at.

He was leaving tonight?!? What kind of bollocks bullshit

nonsense is that? TOnight?! TONIGHT? How? How did he think he was going to feed me, fuck me then just up and leave the country?

Okay, maybe I hadn't woken up and I was still laying on the sofa. I kicked the skirting of my kitchen cupboards and the pain registered in my right foot. I was definitely awake.

'How are you...' I started but I couldn't finish.

The words hadn't formed in my head yet because they kept getting distracted by random sentences and phrases like: WHAT THE FUCK, HOW COULD YOU DO THIS TO ME AND FOR FUCK'S SAKE!

Opening the drawer, I stared at my cutlery.

There was no point stopping the tears.

'This was the hardest thing to tell you. I even changed my flight from this morning to later tonight so I could spend the day with you.'

OH COME ON ANDRE... STOP TALKING MAH G!

Why was he saying sweet shit like that when he was telling me he was leaving me in the same sentence?

My head was shaking of its own accord and I couldn't stop it. Angry words were building in my heart and my arms were shaking. I was folding my toes and drumming my fingers, trying to decide which spoon I was going to make my drink with.

He stepped closer to my back and I got tense.

His energy was pounding my back but his words were keeping us apart. I could tell he didn't know how to touch me.

Obviously, it means more to him than just getting some. I mean if he didn't care he would've got on the first flight and done. But he changed it. He changed to a later flight so he could spend the day with me. Does that sound like someone who didn't want me?

I was still undecided which spoon to use.

A whiff of roses hit me from the left.

TONIGHT?!

There was so much I kept coming back to. He was leaving tonight, he changed the time of the flight, he tried to tell me a few days ago, he gave me the best fucking Valentines day in history and he was leaving me?

And that's when it hit me. He was leaving me!

No more Andre. Oh, wow, the tears are killing me.

Pulling a few sheets of kitchen towel for my eyes, I held my hand over my face.

'Are you okay?' he asked, hovering behind me.

GUYS - this is the worst question question to ask at a time like this. He has to know that I'm not okay. Why would I be? The best dick of my life was suddenly leaving me - tonight apparently - for six fucking months. And he was asking if I was okay? Sure I'm okay, just leave your dick and you can do whatever the fuck you want. I mean all he was doing was standing there but I could feel him. Inside me. It's like I could hear him thinking behind me. He wanted to touch me. He probably wanted to slide his hands around my waist the way he liked to do and nuzzle his chin in my neck.

And I STILL hadn't chosen a spoon. It's not like I own ten thousand teaspoons. But that wasn't what was drawing my attention.

'I mean it's ONLY six months...'

I raised my index finger and showed it to him to stop his

words.

He needed to stop saying shit like that like it was meant to make me feel better. Yeah he could say it's only six months but I would say: it's only SIX MONTHS!

My whole body was shaking.

'Yeah but it's six months that you won't be here.'

I didn't know what else to say. I was writing and rewriting sentences in my head. Fighting with emotion, reason, protection of my feelings, thinking about why the L-word was swimming around... blaaaaaaah.

'But I'm coming back, right?'

'Maybe,' I was fiddling with the drawer handle and pouting. 'I don't know.'

His hands began to creep around my waist and it was like I was electrically charged. My spine straightened, my neck extended and I sighed like he was the answer. There was no question but he WAS the answer.

'For fuck's sake...' I whispered into the air.

'I'm coming back next month for a week so we can...'

'Stop it!'

I was struggling to think. Not that I was struggling but I was thinking too much. Plus his words and his voice and his energy and his smell and his everything kept distracting me. Words became mute but the melody of his voice was still there and I started to sway as his body closed the space between us.

'Spend a whole week together and...'

'Annnnnndre...'

This guy was killing me! You don't even know! I was

gripping onto the drawer like I was trying to pull it straight through the counter. Cutlery clattered and I slammed it shut then opened it again in frustration.

'I know how we started but this is...'

'SO WHY ARE YOU LEAVING ME?'

That's when I lost it. I spun around and beat my hands into his chest, letting everything out. I'd been holding it all in for what felt like forever and he just kept on talking and I just lost it. His arms slowly died around me and fell by his side and he looked at my ceiling with his eyes rolled back.

'Who is gonna fuck me now? Huh?'

Tears were all over my face, even above my eyes for fuck's sake. I must've looked a mess. Frustration built in my chest so quickly, I hit Andre a few more times and he just took the hits. God, even hitting his chest created a flashback and I remembered the mornings waking up on that same chest.

Andre stepped away from me and tilted backwards and collapsed.

Something was wrong because he didn't put his arms behind him to break his fall.

'What the...'

And that's when I saw the taser in my hand!

'OH SHIT!'

The taser in my drawer, next to my teaspoons. The taser I was staring at while Andre was talking and confusing my brain. The taser I bought during my Tatiana Blue research that I stole from the office.

I was curious. I'd never seen a real taser before, let alone used one.

But when the fuck did I pick it up? I was holding onto the drawer but I didn't remember picking it up. I didn't want to hurt him... fuck!

'Andre? Shiiiiiit...'

I rushed over to him and put my hands on his chest, checking his airways and his pulse. My tears were streaming and I cupped his face, trying to scream him awake. His chest was moving but he wasn't waking up.

And then the electricity died!

Straight pitch fucking black!

I screamed and felt completely lost. What crap to have to deal with while dealing with the fact that I just knocked Andre out by accident.

Yes accident, come on, I 'm not crazy!

DISCLAIMER: I have been asked NOT to write about what happened next.

Thursday 15th February 2018

A headache hit me first. Then pain. Then more pain.

I opened my eyes and the first thing my eyes focussed on was my second, lighter pillow. The one I usually put between my thighs when I missed...

'ANDRE!?' I screamed out.

Big mistake. Headache remember?

Wincing and laying on my front I groaned my arms under me and pushed myself up. I felt like I'd slept for a week and a minute at the same time. Sort of rested but tired at the same time you know?

'ANDRE?!?!'

Closing my eyes and squeezing them as hard as I could, I waited for the pain to register in my head and braced. It came over and hovered over me like a rain cloud and passed slowly.

I slid off my bed onto woozy feet and wobbled out of my bedroom.

'What the fuck is wrong with my legs?'

In the corridor: silence.

Looking left and right, there was nothing moving, no music playing.

'ANDRE?!'

I braced for the pain.

Five seconds standing still, I shuffled to the living room and looked at my wall clock.

It was 10:18am, 15th of February.

My living room was exactly the way I left it. Flowers in a vase on my middle table. 'Where is he? Where's my phone? What the fuck?'

Twisting on a confused pivot, I traced my steps.

Oh don't worry, they've gone now, I'm gonna tell you every fucking thing, just let me find my phone.

Bedroom. Night-stand. Charging hopefully.

I unlocked my phone and called Brina straight away.

She was the first and only person I needed to speak to at this moment.

Why, you ask?

Well, I haven't heard from her since that morning when she "fucked" Andre to scratch an itch. Which didn't actually happen by the way. But, she is also the fucking reason why I couldn't finish the last chapter properly. And probably the reason why Andre isn't here right now.

Her number rang as I turned on the TV and walked into the kitchen to turn the kettle on. This was a straight coffee moment.

Flowers again.

My feet walked on the same place when Andre was laying last night just before everything went to shit and I sighed. I put my phone on speaker next to the coffee and stretched my back.

'FUCKING ANSWER YOUR PHONE!' I shouted.

It rang out and went to her voicemail. I hung up and called again.

She was NOT hiding from me any more.

Oh, yeah, well… remember, last night when I accidentally tasered Andre after he said he was leaving me?

Okay, when I say it like that it sounds crazy but I swear to you it was an accident. I HONESTLY didn't do it on purpose, I don't even remember picking it up. I don't even know why it was in there in the first place. I truly don't.

Anyway, so while I was dealing that, there was a fucking blackout.

Yeah I know. Or at least what I thought was a blackout.

It was not that!

Last night I met the…

'Hey sis,' Brina cheerfully said.

I picked up phone and held it in front of my face.

'WHAT THE FUCK DID YOU DO?'

'The right thing it seems like.'

'How… no, no, no… When did… no, not even. Why did

you do this?'

'One word sis: dickmatised!'

'If you say that word to me one more fucking time...'

'Sis, I know you don't believe in it or you think that it's just something that people talk about and that's fine. But, Andre GOT you!'

'Got me how?'

'Hooked!'

'HOW?'

'Did you or did you not tase the boy after he told you he had to leave? Yes or no?'

'Listen, I know you already know the answer to that question.'

'Yes I DO know the answer to that question which is why I'm asking you.'

'Did they let you see the video?'

'Yep!'

'So you saw that I didn't do it on purpose right?'

I spooned three full spoons of coffee into an extra large cup.

'Listen, I'm not calling you to talk about whether you did that on purpose or not... It WAS a little weird but hey, to each their own. I just wanted to tell you why I did it.'

'Where is he?'

'They put him on his flight.'

'For fuck's sake!'

'What did you WANT them to do, leave him for you?'

YES!

'No, of course not I wanted him to go!'

'Is that why you hit him with a taser Simone?'

'It was AN ACCIDENT!'

'Anyway, the reason why I called The C.L.I.T.S on you is because I wasn't the only one who thought Andre got you too. Katrina and Russia agreed with me. You've been missing from the group, you're changing, you look different, you're not taking care of yourself. This is an important time for you and you're letting some dick distract you.'

'Hold on, who the fuck are you to tell ME about my life? Huh? Sorry but where did your husband sleep last night? Do you even know?'

'I don't know and I don't care, I've left him!'

'What?! When? Don't chat shit, you didn't leave Donovan.'

'I did!'

'Where are you?'

'I'm... out!'

I needed to bring focus back to this conversation.

'Sis, you called The C.L.I.T.S on me? First of all, I didn't...'

'Do you know what one of them said to me? She said that you are one of the worst cases of dick addiction she's ever seen.'

Hot water spilled on the counter near my phone and I moved it quickly.

'Fuck... Really? One of the worst cases? Come on!'

'That's what she said. But you know what The C.L.I..T.S do... they support women to make sure we shine and men don't fuck with us. Andre was fucking with you.'

'No, Andre was FUCKING ME!'

'Raw too!'

'What?'

I stuttered on myself. How did she know that?

'Don't play dumb, I know okay.'

'What do you know?'

Of course I played dumb, I didn't want her to lecture me and tell me what I didn't want to hear.

'Sim, I know!'

I sighed. 'Did he get off okay?'

'I think so, they told me he got on it but I don't know.'

This was the thing I couldn't talk about. They made me not write about it but they're fucking gone now so I can say whatever the fuck I want!

Last night was MAD real! While I was trying to wake Andre up and the lights went out, that's when the scariest shit happened. The electricity came back on, lights back on and there were six black women sitting on my sofa. No lie, real talk, six random black women on my sofa. I stared at them for so long because I didn't think I was seeing what I was seeing but I was seeing what I was seeing. And then one of them said 'hey Simone'.

I was SHIT scared! First of all, how the fuck did they get in? It's not like I left the door open. And how did they get in so quick? And they were sitting on my sofa like they'd been here before. It was the weirdest, strangest, most surreal thing I've ever seen in my life.

These six women, each of them stunning by the way, was looking at me holding Andre's unconscious face like they knew something I didn't. At that point I didn't know a thing!

So, last night I met The Genesis, Roro The Lady, Nikki Vixxen, Marquita The Teacher, Myatta and Zeah The Ball Crusher. If those names mean nothing to you then there's a lot of shit you don't know. These are C.L.I.T.S names. You know The C.L.I.T.S? Clever Ladies Investigating Terrible Situations? Legendary group of black women who kidnap and torture men in order to teach them to be better? Operating for over 12 years without being caught? No?

I know OF them but I'd never met any of them. I came across them during my Tatiana Blue research and that was all I knew. Like Tatiana Blue, they were legends, myths, people you heard about but never knew anyone who encountered them. Sure there were stories of men disappearing in the middle of the night and reappearing a week later in different mind frames but, again, legend.

Lemme tell you something, that legend is real.

'Hello? Are you still there?' Brina said on the phone.

'Hold on...'

So yeah, they were just sitting on my sofa and one of them, I think she was the leader, she proceeded to break down who they were and what they were doing there. Basically, Brina called them and told them that she was worried about me and that she thought I was dickmatised. Not only dickmatised but ignorant to it too. This made her worry and she reached out to them, who'd been watching me since day one. DAY ONE YA KNOW? That's how she knew.

Anyway, they sat me down and told me about some the worst cases of dick addiction they had seen. From what I knew, I didn't think that was something they did but apparently it was. They told me about a case of addicktion where a women paid another man's rent in the same block of flats that she lived in with her partner of 11 years all because of good dick. Or the other woman who gave her good dick a key to her place and moved him in then almost killed him when he got married to someone else.

Horror stories, absolute horror stories but I didn't think any of them were me. I hadn't lost control, I hadn't delved into the depths of madness where I refusing to come out, happy to live in the mire of Andre's manliness. He didn't have me under lock and key where he controlled my movements and I had no space to exist as I did before I met him. I was just happy to fuck him… to let him fuck me.

That's all.

So, the ladies proceeded to detail the exact moments in the last 14 days where I've displayed moments of change or momentary indecision which were attributed Andre's presence in my life. And let me tell you, they had camera footage of us everywhere. The hotel, my bathroom, my bedroom, my kitchen…

'HELLOOO?' Brina shouted, reminding me she was there.

'I really can't believe you did this to me. The dick was soooo…'

'That's exactly why I did this to you!'

'Yeah but…'

'When did they leave?'

'I have no idea. I don't remember going to bed but that's where I woke up. Got up and everything was back to normal. I STILL don't think I was dickmatised you know.'

'Awww sis, I did you a favour.'

With my drink in hand, I shuffled to my spot on the sofa, remembering the woman with the dreadlocks who sat in my spot last night. Then I thought about the time I was talking on Skype and Andre ate my pussy there too.

'FUCK'S SAKE!'

Last one I swear. I flicked to E4.

Yeah, last night was a madness. I took a sip of my drink and burnt my lips.

My eyes drifted up to the TV and I froze.

'Oh. My. God! Oh MY God... Ohmygodohmygodohmygod OH MY GOD!'

I put my drink on the table and shook my hand like it burned, my eyes glued to the screen. Scrambling for the remote, I turned the volume up all the way.

'THE ADVERT FOR MY DOCUMENTARY IS ON! AHHHHHHHHH!'

I didn't know there was an advert. I'd spoken to my managers who were thinking about an advert but I didn't know there was one.

'Congratulations sis.'

I was dancing around the room at this point. I immediately wanted Andre to press me against the windows with London below. Survey the town I was about to takeover kind of thing.

'For fuck's sake Andre... I mean thanks sis!' My sarcasm was clear.

Okay, THAT'S the last one, I swear.

OoOoOooo... coming soon!

The trailer had a beautiful high-heeled ending and I was literally on the edge of my seat. Like literally balanced on the edge of my sofa.

'Oh wow, that was like sex.'

Well not like sex with Andre. Sex with Andre was not like

anything of this world. No food, no drink, no purchase, NOTHING was like sex with Andre. That was magic and sorcery, mixed with Sunset rum, unicorns and Amsterdam weed.

'Alright I'm gone. I've explained my shit.'

'Wait, no, you can't just go.'

'Listen, you've had you're fun with some dick, now it's my time!'

'Where ARE you?'

I was mixed up. The excitement of my advert was coursing through me, the strangeness of meeting actual members of The C.L.I.T.S was still present, Andre's presence practically emanated off me and I missed him. I know he had to go and do his thing and I didn't try to make him stay by tasering him and making him miss his flight.

I know no-one said it but I know you're thinking it. And that's fine, I know the truth.

'Simone... well done on your advert. I'll see you in a few days.'

'What do you mean a few days? I'm not done with you yet... you've ruine...'

She hung up before I finished talking. Tossing my phone, I sighed.

I sat back on my sofa and kicked my legs up, excited about the advert but also wishing I could've gotten The C.L.I.T.S to comment for the documentary. With my thumb in my mouth, Andre's thoughts clouded over everything and I missed him like never before. I'd never thought about how we would end but I didn't see it ending like this. I don't think I ever thought about our thing ending in any way that meant I wasn't going to get some more.

I know, not the best ending to a story but yeah, that's it I guess.

I'm dick-less once again.

Story of my life.

Meanwhile...

Brina hung up her phone and laid back on crisp clean sheets. She felt like she'd tied up all loose ends and was okay to relax.

In her heart of hearts she knew she did what she did for the right reasons and she was looking out for her sister. It's what she always did as big sister. Ever since they lost their mum, Brina became the force of the family and her main priority was looking after Simone.

Looking around, she closed her dressing gown and hugged it to her chest.

She gave Donovan a thought and he was gone just as fast.

Her phone rang again.

Looking at the display with a smile, she answered and rolled onto her stomach, kicking her legs.

'Well hello you...'

'Hey,' Andre said. 'My flight should be coming in early so I shouldn't be that much longer. How you enjoying Japan?'

'I'll enjoy it more when you're here.'

'Yeah you will.'

The End...

Books by Mr Oh:

Little Black Book Volume One
Little Black Book Volume Two
Little Black Book Volume Three
The Tall Tales of Tatiana Blue

Shorts by Mr Oh:

L&I
The Train
7 Floors

Please enjoy this snippet from my next book, The League of Chocolate Gentlemen

REECE - 23rd February, 22:25pm

His search for the right outfit consisted of looking through his clean and dirty clothes, though he seemed to have more of the latter. A broken drum in his washing machine and a £300 repair fee meant his drum stayed broken and the laundrette saw him sporadically.

By the time he found an outfit and gave it a long sniff and a press with the iron on his bed, he was late. Again.

He topped up his Oyster Card and got on the Central line to Leytonstone. The vibe of the train was jovial as a large group of women were laughing with a woman with a veil and an L plate on her back and chest.

Jumping off the train and onto a bus, Reece had five minutes to reach his destination which was ten minutes away. His penchant for being late was something he didn't want to exercise tonight but, in his mind, being five minutes late was a sign of growth and improvement.

The bus pulled up to the stop and Reece was the first one off the bus. He looked up at the Sir Alfred Hitchcock hotel and was in awe. He'd been past the hotel many times but had never stopped to admire the building which looked like a medieval castle with front and back parking.

A crisp breeze whooshed past him in the open space and he pulled the collar of his cardigan up. Another well-dressed black man turned to pass him and walked towards the hotel.

'Must be the place,' he said to himself and followed

behind the man in the suit.

Bollards and safety tape were present around parts of the building as he walked up rickety wooden steps. The closer he got to the open doors of the entrance, the more he could hear laughter and deep voices.

'Hello... Reece is it?'

Hearing his name from a voice he didn't recognise made him spin around. With no one behind him, he was spinning around until he caught the sight of a hand in the air.

'Over here!'

A black man with six different piercings on his face looked at Reece with a smile from behind a reception counter.

'Reece?'

'Er... Yeah?' he said, looking at the receptionist with an single scowling eyebrow raised. His "gaydar" gave him an instant alert.

'Hi. Just wanted to mark you in. Food is through there. Valerie is running late but she'll be out in a second. Go through.'

He nodded his head and turned to the low hum of male voices he could hear. In the large conference room he came face-to-face with a sea of black men in all shades, shapes and pay packets judging by their different clothes, ranging from suits to jeans and one guy chomping a chicken bone in a velour tracksuit.

'Is this thing on?' said Valerie's voice through the speakers. 'Good evening gentlemen. Thank you for coming.'

QUÉ - 23rd February, 22:33pm

After counting the piercings on the receptionist's face, he took off his jacket and walked in on Valerie taking the stage.

'As I've said to all of you, I've brought you here to talk about an business opportunity.'

She was dressed in a long white summer dress with no bra and thick Janet Jackson braids that ran down her back. Over her ear, she wore a wireless microphone and was pacing the stage, talking to a room full of black men.

'Now, take a look at the man standing right next to you. That man has done what you've done. Me! Now we've dealt with the elephant in the room, I want you to look at me and think about this. Football teams.'

Qué was scanning the crowd, looking back to Valerie who clearly wasn't wearing any underwear. He didn't recognise any of the faces of Valerie's other side pieces and there were a lot.

'Premier league. First place takes the league, second place and third place. Now imagine you are the team at the top. What would you win? What about second place? Or third?'

Valerie was using her skills as a public speaker to hold the crowd. Her TV personality meant she knew when and how to use her hands, when to pause her sentences and when to let her words marinate amongst the crowd.

'I'm starting a league. A league of chocolate gentlemen. I'll bring you some of the sexiest, most powerful women in the country and I want you to fuck them. I want you to do what you've done to me. And I want you to do it again and again and again. The more you make them cum, the more points you win. Get more orgasms than the man next to you and win the league. And you win. Big.'

Qué made his way to the table of food and he could see catered cultural treats. Macaroni and cheese cupcakes, slices of cornbread, small ackee and saltfish dumplings and miniature cups of jollof rice.

'First place wins a £1 million house in Chelsea and £500,000.'

The room of men all perked up at the same time. Qué's eyes widened and watched as Valerie grinned sexily at the men who were all glaring at her with pound signs in their eyes.

'Second place takes a £500,000 apartment in Shoreditch and £100,000 and third place gets a £250,000 flat in Islington. Fourth and fifth get their rent or mortgages paid for a year. All you have to do to win is sleep with a woman or three or four. And you get £100 to start. How does that sound?'

Murmurs and excited hums of approval sounded throughout the room as Valerie held her hands out, giving an open invitation to stare at her nipples which were imprinted against her dress.

'Don't answer now. Enjoy the food, there's an open bar so drink up and you'll find something in your email. Reply to it and let's make one of you some money.'

Qué spotted Reece's excited eyes from across the room. Valerie left the stage without talking to anyone but all eyes watched her leave.

REECE - 26th February, 2:56am

His laptop was open as the world slept around him. Cars speeding past his windows were few and far between as he sat with a notepad to his right and a bowl of pineapple rings to his left. Multiple tabs were open on his Google Chrome page; some playing videos, some giving information and others taking up space.

Reece received his email from Valerie two hours ago and he was already researching positions and foods to make his sperm taste better. His search in a new tab was about a practice he'd heard about called 'edging' but he wanted to know more.

The tart sting of the pineapple rings on his tongue made his brow furrow down as he watched a video of a man masturbating then stopping when he was about cum. Reece looked confused.

'Why would you do that?' he asked the video. 'Just let the ting buss innit!?'

As he read on, feeling awkward watching a man masturbate, he switched tabs to a video of a man with his face between a woman's thighs while talking at the same time.

'...now every woman likes her pussy eaten differently. My wife here, she likes a mix of having her clit licked, not flicked. Licked. And she also likes her G-Spot reached. Now not everyone has the tongue length to reach such a spot but that's okay, you can use a finger too.'

Reece was never scared of going down on women but he grew to become one of those 'man don't do them tings'. The more proficient he became with his dick, the less he spent exploring with his tongue. By that point, he joined the 'man don't do dem tings' crew fully and swore it out of his sexual performance completely. Though he secretly enjoyed it.

'Might need to bring it back if I'm gonna win this ting... Yeah but there were some tonks dudes in there,' he said to himself. 'Chaaa... Let me just do me.'

He went back to the tab of Valerie's email and looked over the rules again, becoming more aroused at the thought of what was to come.

Opening another tab, he went to Valerie's property website and looked at her company's refurbishment jobs on different properties throughout the country. Like Kirsty Allsopp, she was a fan of knocking through a wall but her visions of greatness would always come through in the end and she could convince anyone that her way was the best way. Her portfolio of over 1,000 sold homes blurred as he scrolled through her properties from under £1,000 to her crowning glory £6 million house in Kensington that she sold to Tinie Tempah for £9 million.

'Imagine... Me and lil' man could have our boys room and watch football...'

The thought of his son angered him as visions of his son's mum drew a veil of red over his vision. Reece tried to calculate how he could fuck his way to being a better father.

'Focus fam...'

At that moment, another email came in from Valerie announcing the official start of The League of Chocolate Gentlemen. Below the introduction was a time, date and location for his first appointment. The game had begun.

#0055 - 250518 - C0 - 210/148/9 - PB - DID2206052